FISH
COUGH

A NOVEL

CRAIG BUCHNER

Praise for Fish Cough

Craig Buchner has written a strange and powerful novel, a story that flares and zooms at the reader like the meteor shower that dazzles and bewilders our heroes, Thom and Howard. For all its otherworldly aspects, *Fish Cough* is a story about animals trying to make sense of the chaos around, and inside them, about love as the ultimate force of disequilibrium, and the ultimate source of hope. Brilliant.

Steve Almond, author of
All the Secrets of the World

Meteorites and great fires, pet squirrels and bottle caps with secret codes, good and evil, drama and comedy, anger and grief and love, yes, mostly love, like the works of George Saunders or Lorrie Moore that depict the warped madness of these modern times as a means for us to see ourselves clearer, Craig Buchner's *Fish Cough* is a wildly imaginative, deeply thoughtful, and potently-moving riot of a novel.

Alan Heathcock, author of *VOLT* and *40*

Fish Cough is a strikingly original fable of apocalypse that surprises by its focus on ordinary life – the way we continue to love and struggle to find meaning and connection even in the midst of the End. It rang very true to me.

Dan Chaon, author of *Sleepwalk*

Buckman Publishing LLC
1033 SE Main Suite 4
Portland OR 97214
buckmanpublishing.com

Fish Cough/ Craig Buchner

ISBN: 979-8-9854927-4-3
Library of Congress Control Number: 2022946734

Hello from Portland, Oregon, U.S.A

For Delphine

Prologue

Smoke shaped like a fish head hung over the warehouse. Pumper trucks and police cruisers flashed red and blue strobe lights, and volunteer firefighters crisscrossed the lot with choreographed precision. The blaze had been extinguished from the loading dock—all that remained. Soon the wind picked up, unanchoring the coal-black smoke, the fish head cloud making glacial progress. It would soon dissolve into thin air as if it had never existed.

We lived in a strange world where alien objects fell from the sky and buildings could suddenly vanish. That was what had happened.

It was the first meteorite of the shower to pass through the atmosphere and touch down. At the time, no one knew that the golf ball-sized rock, by the time it pierced the transformer box on the utility pole, had once been a part of a meteoroid that measured three hundred thirty-three feet across and had traveled sixty-two million miles. At the time, no one knew that the blast of sparks caused by the meteoroid fragment zipping through the energized equipment would ignite the brittle gray leaves on the overhanging oak tree and eventually drop a small, flaming branch onto the roof of the warehouse where the maintenance crew had retarred and graveled a six square feet patch to prevent a leak, the spark causing a swift and brutal fire that raced across the surface and eventually ate its way through to the second floor's ceiling and into each room below. At the time, no one knew that the jet-black stone, as glossy as a bead of beluga caviar, that was wedged into the base of the oak tree would be the cause of so much strangeness.

Book I

Chapter 1

He looked at me for the first time in two days.

I said, "I care about you. I want us to make each other happy. I just don't know if we do anymore."

Howard hesitated. Then he nodded. This was good. We were communicating. The pinched hole of his mouth moved slowly. It wasn't a smile but a glimmer. There had to be a cure for whatever was happening between us. Howard wanted something from this relationship that I wasn't budging on—a child. In return, I wanted something that Howard held back.

Had our relationship turned into a chess match?

"I wish we could start over," I said. "What was it even like? In the beginning."

I know we played our moves wrong, but I wanted to try again.

Every Thursday, Crush—the closest bar to our apartment—hosted trivia night. A weekly get-together for Howard and his trivialist cohort that predated our time.

In the beginning, he'd tell me the questions his team missed. Coming home half-cocked, he'd say, "Thom, did you know that fourteen percent of people think cilantro tastes like soap?"

He'd say, "Our country was named after Amerigo Vespucci."

He'd say, "The human body contains nine pints of blood."

But tonight, like the night before, he didn't say a word when he got home. Tonight, someone else spoke first.

"Thommy Salami," Antonio said, pulling me into a bear hug.

He'd been our guest before, but this was the first time in a long time. Hair on his chest spilling out of his V-neck. Hot, stale breath on my ear as he said, "You smell magnifico."

But he smelled like cigarettes and gin.

Howard shrugged and held up his palms. A classic "Don't ask me" gesture.

"Everyone drinking?" Antonio asked.

I poured whiskey into Howard's silver-rimmed tumblers. The metal was faded from the dishwasher.

"Congrats on getting engaged," I said, still wondering why Howard brought him home.

"Oh, that," he said. "That one didn't stick. But congrats to you both," Antonio continued. "Half a decade together. But Howard says you need a little variété. And with this, what is it called, the lion-something. That meteor shower, right, maybe a big ole rock is going to wipe us out like the dinosaurs. So, for tonight, let's all carpe diem."

"The Leonids," I said. "That's the name of it."

"Yes, that's exactly it," Antonio said. "Maybe none of us have much time if the worst… well."

Howard grimaced. "What do you say?" he was talking only to me.

"I mean," I said. "I'm not opposed."

Then Howard grabbed Antonio's belt. Until recently, Howard considered himself a top. We blamed his inability to perform on stress: we made too little money, we worked too many hours, we planned too many evenings. Routine killed romance.

This was all so unlike Howard.

"Finally," Antonio said, reaching for me. He found that spot on my neck to kiss.

Down on his knees, Howard unzipped my jeans, then he backed away slowly like a bombmaker who had just triggered something of unfathomable power.

Without saying a word, he waited for us to start.

I wondered what an animal watching us through the window would think of us sweating and grunting. It was all for pure pleasure, although that wasn't entirely true. It was to pretend our sex life was something else. Something that hadn't vanished.

Howard left us. I didn't hear him anywhere.

Antonio grabbed my hips as I lowered onto his lap. I pushed down, and Antonio lifted me. I bucked back. He heaved again, but I put him in his place. He tried again, but I wouldn't let him. Forced him into me. Now. This time together. Uncontainable energy building. I sensed the familiarity of coming. I did it to him.

His hands released my hips, and I felt him unload.

But I kept going.

"Thommy," he said. "Thom! Stop."

But I didn't, and I slammed against him. I wanted it back. Howard and I. Our past. Our youth. All of it. But it was gone, and this was the last of it. A few teaspoons of sweat and cum from another man. I went berserk. I wanted to break him off. When this ends, it all ends.

"Jesus, man, stop!" Antonio said.

He shoved my hips, and breathlessly I apologized; but I wasn't sorry.

I fell onto the bed next to him.

I said, "I got carried away."

"No kidding," Antonio said, searching for his clothes.

Howard returned, looking at the mess of sheets and shirts and socks.

"Where were you?" I asked.

"I need to get going," Antonio said.

"You don't want another drink?" I asked.

When the house was quiet, Howard and I stripped the bed. Together we tucked the clean sheets under the mattress and fluffed the comforter. Howard slid under the covers first.

"It wasn't like it used to be," I said.

Howard shook his head.

I said, "This wasn't only about me. You did this for you, too, right?"

But he looked away. He wasn't shy; he just didn't want to admit the real reason.

"You didn't even want to try?"

He pulled the blankets to his chin like a child too nervous to speak. I slid my hand down his chest.

"Let me give it a go," I said.

He closed his eyes and bit his lip, as my fingers swam through his pubic hair. I gave him a tug. Then another.

"What is it?" I asked. "Does it feel good or no?"

Howard shook his head. Was that a tear on his cheek?

"I don't think it's a bad thing," I said, resting my hand on his stomach.

He nodded—trying to agree with me.

I kissed his cheek and held my face against his. But he was frozen. Like a block of ice. I wanted to save him. To thaw him out. But this was all we had. This moment. Because this was the last moment it was ever this good—and it wasn't good at all.

Chapter 2

Five years earlier we named our apartment. Affectionately known as "the Pit Stop," the nickname predating our marriage when it was still illegal for two men to stand in front of a justice of the peace and say the words, "I do."

We lived a ten-minute walk from Crush, the only gay bar in Southeast Portland, and from Crush you walked east on Morrison Street, passing Floyd's Coffee Shop, King Harvest Drive-Thru Hummus—home of the *Wednesday $2 Hummus Burrito*—and Divine Moments Tattoo Parlor, located on the ground floor of our building. Around the back was an entrance, a single green door in a splintered frame that led to a narrow stairwell and our apartment.

Our living room faced south over Morrison, above Divine Moments, looking at a warehouse. I'd spent too many afternoons ignoring my own work and wondering what went on in that warehouse. People, men mostly, and trucks would come and go, but I never saw anything being produced. Instead, I invented stories about what those men did in that warehouse: mass-producing lifelike sex dolls or hosting cosplay conventions or filming music videos. But it was likely far less interesting. Bulk merchandise storage. Or machine parts.

The bedroom, on the west side, snuggled the neighbors' building, while our kitchen on the east was windowless and subway tiled black and white. Working from home meant I spent too much time in this space, so I'd imagine our rooms decorated with our neighbors' Eames chairs and teak dressers and a Kosta Boda vase centered on a salvaged wood coffee table. The equivalent of stacking thousands of dollars in a pile, just to admire.

In this space, I wrote articles about Portland for a Portland magazine named after Portland. I liked the research, learning the *when* about the city. Like when our building was constructed. 1908. And I enjoyed the *what*, too. Because in 1908 our apartment was originally the location of a doctor's office. Exploring city records and blueprints, I learned our living room and kitchen had been the waiting room. And our bedroom, such a plain room, was where the doctor had doctored.

No one would ever guess it had any history at all based on the cream painted walls and polished pine floor, the simple white window frames and dimpled ceiling. None of it said "doctor," not like today's offices with recessed lighting and Tristan crown molding and the unconsciously chosen artwork of a schooner on a rolling sea—a painting like that centered high on the wall as if owning such a lavish piece of noncommittal art reflected the doctor's superior powers of healing broken bones and destroying budding cancer cells.

Instead, our apartment—an Ikea-furnished one-bedroom—resembled a pit stop, a place to retrieve a prescription of Amoxicillin or sit for a swift but secure gauze-wrap for a sprained wrist. A short layover, which was more or less how Howard and I used the space.

Except we didn't seek medical help in those early days of our romance; we sought sexual healing.

Although we didn't know one another in our twenties, those years provided each of us with enough sexual experiences and experimentation, most of which did more damage than good—if not to our bodies then our minds. Because sex was a weapon used for good and evil. We can all recall those sexual enemies, the ones we no longer call by name but instead only refer to by their code words.

"The German."

"Mr. Perfect Smile."

"Antonio's sketchy friend."

Now in our thirties, we were especially in need of sexual

16

healing. The affirmation that another man could love me, and I could wake up tomorrow and he would still be there. That after falling into his arms, I could tell him every secret in my head—every weird thought—and he wouldn't use those stories against me as examples of my malfunctioning brain.

But Howard and I had long grown out of our lean years and were now pleasantly rooted in another phase of life. Having eased out of our "pit stop" phase, our bodies now softer, hairier, less responsive, we were entering our "flatlining" phase. Missing an evening together didn't feel like the threat to our bond it once did. Instead, in my hours alone, my mind would fill each gap with fantasies about other men. Meeting someone at a café or having a fling in Europe. I knew I was just pining for the early days of our relationship when Howard found everything about me exciting.

Five years into our relationship, was I thinking about ending things or just breaking some of the rules?

Chapter 3

Freelance assignments appeared like magic before our bank accounts dipped into negative territory. That was the best way to describe the ebb and flow of our finances. There was always an urgent sense of work that kept us tense.

But I couldn't focus, and I was tired of reading articles about the Leonids. Every reporter with a thought said their piece about the meteor shower—a once every thirty-three and a half years occurrence. Some thought it would amount to something akin to the most spectacular fireworks show ever, brought to us by the cosmos, while others feared the planet was in jeopardy of being pounded by an army of intergalactic projectiles. They speculated that it only took one giant asteroid to wipe out the dinosaurs, and that a few thousand smaller meteors might replicate that amount of damage, creating enough soot upon impact that it would cloud the sky and block out the sun.

No matter what website I went to, journalists quoted scientists about the very real possibility that we were about to enter a second mass extinction. I could only doom scroll for so long before I shut my laptop. But that was the news these days–everything had to be unprecedented.

I gazed out the window and watched a chubby squirrel race around the sidewalk, sneaking past Malala, the neighborhood cat, and crawl through the grass and hardy palms and sweetspire. The squirrel stopped and stood on two legs, looking around. A diamond of white fur on his chest. I never really paid attention to squirrels, but there was something strange about this squirrel. Beyond the diamond. There was something about the way he moved. He had an awareness that other wildlife lacked. But Howard would tell me I was projecting. That there wasn't some great power locked away. That the meaning I was finding was the meaning I was creating. Maybe he was right.

Still, there was an attractive element to nature that I couldn't deny. Not the nature that was a destructive meteor shower but the simple nature of a small furry creature going about his day. Foraging. Frolicking. I envied the squirrel. Having his own thoughts, even if they weren't complex, but still thoughts that were entirely separate from the human world.

Somehow, I had entangled myself in a life of bills and deadlines and taxes and expectations, and I could never not think of those things. A part of me secretly hoped that the Leonids would cause enough damage to reset the world. Make people realize that life was short. That our current system wasn't working. Why did we have to work so hard to get so little in return? Maybe I secretly wanted to become that squirrel with the beautiful diamond on his chest.

I whistled to him, and he climbed the vines along our building to our windowsill, but when the doorbell rang, the squirrel chattered nervously. Something about the way he looked at me, his dark, penetrating eyes, said, "Don't answer."

But this was our home, our safe space.

I closed the window and answered the door. Two teenage boys wearing matching blue sport coats.

"Hello, sir," they said in unison. "Do you believe the world needs better rules?"

"I'm sorry?" I asked.

They weren't twins, but they were the same height. The same noses. But different hair.

"Do you believe we're all in the path of a devasting storm?" the red-haired boy said. He was clearly the leader of the two, standing slightly closer to me.

"I'm not sure I'd call it that," I said.

"If you and… Are you married, sir?" he asked. "It's easier if we speak to everyone at once."

He was very polite.

"I am married," I said, appreciating his politeness.

"If you and your wife have a moment, we would like to talk to you about a very special promise we can make. There's so much to talk about with what might happen in the coming weeks, we're here to share that there's a plan." He smiled on cue. As if trained. "A great kingdom has been built, and we're here because we've reserved a spot for you and your wife."

But I stopped him. "Husband," I said.

"I'm sorry?" the red-haired boy asked; he was now confused on how to proceed.

"Me and my husband. You were saying there's room left for my husband and I?"

The other boy—the one with the cleft lip and straw-colored hair—stared, unblinking.

The leader started again, trying to regain composure. "The storm. We can't just get out of its path. But we can help protect you and your wife."

"Husband," I repeated. "There is no wife here. Only men."

The boy with the cleft said, "Maybe we're in the wrong place, Brax."

Brax nodded.

"Are you sure?" I asked. "Because I don't think you're wrong. Who knows what's going to happen with the meteors? It's been on the news around the clock. We'd love for you to tell us."

"Sorry," Brax said, and looked at his partner. His wide eyes asking, *What do we do?*

"Thank you for your time," his second-in-command said. "We're not trained for this."

Somehow one word was enough to end the conversation. With the weight of the world ending upon us, too. I repeated that word in my head.

Of the words that could shake a person, *husband* never crossed my mind.

Chapter 4

I dreamed of a black cat in the corner of the room. It was a dream I've had before. Sometimes it was a black cat, other times it was a small round body. Like a caterpillar in a cocoon. Once it was a white mouse with beady red eyes. But in every dream, it waited in the corner of the room. Watching me.

I grew up Catholic, but I didn't believe in most of it. The soul, however, seemed conceivable. Unparalleled energy in the body. I could understand that. When the body died, wouldn't that liveliness escape like a sneaking black cat? Moving from a place in the center of your chest to slink away into the corner of the room while the body cooled in the hollow silence. Those were instructions for dying. And in this dream, that was me in bed and that was my soul in the corner of the room. Howard was always beside me. I was never aware if Howard was awake, but I would feel his hand, like a warm animal, slowly move onto mine.

"I can't tell if I'm still sleeping," I said.

I knew I wasn't dreaming any more. I could feel the actual heat of his body, and I could smell our collective breath in the air. Like burnt garlic.

I reached for my phone on the nightstand, but then I didn't. The blue light would wake up the brain.

I said, "Why are you up? Are you thinking about what might happen?"

He groaned a long growl like a beast. Then he rubbed his hips. His father had bone spurs. Howard feared he would inherit all the bad traits from his family. It was a legitimate fear.

"Hips?" I asked.

He sighed, and I pressed my body against him, but he jerked away.

"You probably pulled a muscle," I said, massaging his thigh. Simply touching him aroused me. There was nothing to do about that though. "Or maybe it's stress. I know I haven't been easy lately. There's just so much going on in the world."

Early on in our relationship Howard was our foundation, but this was also Howard—the vulnerable one—the one who was coming apart in front of me.

I said, "Maybe sleep will help. We're both repressed."

Howard angled his head. Even in the dark I could see him.

I yawned, and said, "That's funny. I actually meant depressed."

Of all the things I should regret, I had few. Not meeting strangers from Craigslist, or driving drunk, or being a bad friend. But for five years I've dodged his singularly important question.

When can we start a family?

With everyone talking about the end of the world, I had an even greater sense of clarity. We can't bring someone into our life knowing that everything could instantly be destroyed.

Having a family was what we argued about. For Howard, it was the main goal in life. I couldn't quite understand. He would try to explain it. People who were raised in a positive home environment, like he was, with a stable family, like his, would want to create that life with their significant other. Howard wanted to pass on that joy.

And I wanted that, too. I think.

But we had problems, real problems. A child wasn't going to fix them.

In bed with Howard, I said, "Will a child really fix all this? Your hip problems aren't going to go away. And our stuff, that's not just going to disappear. Plus, what if it's worse than they're saying. What if the sky goes completely black? Then what?"

He looked at me, sadly, like a dog.

"What are you saying?" he asked. "There's always a reason."

"Isn't it bothering you? The world is about to be destroyed, and the only thing on your mind is a kid?"

"Are you okay?" Howard asked.

I knew I shouldn't have said it. This was the conversation we've avoided again and again. He'd bring it up, and I'd dismiss him, change the subject, challenge him. I knew it bothered him. My resistance. Not everyone grew up in a stable environment. Some parents had serious flaws, I wanted to tell him, and it would be unavoidable that those children would not carry on those flaws.

"Howie, I can barely take care of myself. I'd be a horrible father."

It was the middle of the night, and I'd chosen this moment to unpack years of frustration. I don't know why I chose right now, but the words jumped out of me. They floated in the air like anvils hanging on balloons. Waiting to snap and crush someone.

"Thom," he said. "I think you're dreaming. You're sleep talking."

I heard his voice. It was far away, but I rubbed my eyes. Pushing my fingers into them to wake myself up. Hard. Not enough to hurt myself but enough to see phosphenes. In the darkness behind my eyelids were bursts of light. A twinkling, swirling pattern of stars. Then flashes like the Leonids. But when I opened my eyes, the room was still. There was nothing in the corner of the room. No black cat. No soul. But I wasn't alone. Howard was sound asleep beside me. Only inches away. But it seemed like a chasm. Maybe I was alone.

Chapter 5

When I first signed the lease to the apartment, I was single.

I read every clause—a time consuming habit—and when it came to pets, they were forbidden. At the time, it was a non-issue because I was allergic to cats and the notion of owning a dog was impossible and irresponsible in such a small dwelling. Friends adopted dogs and cats, and they weren't shy about lecturing non-pet people on the therapeutic powers of that companionship. Devoting themselves to their purebred pets ranked on a hypothetical scale akin to adopting a refugee child from Syria, but buying an eight-week-old apricot pug for two thousand dollars from a puppy factory in Canby, Oregon, was hardly a humanitarian effort.

Yet maybe a pet was exactly what we needed. Something to squelch his desire for a child.

I lived long enough alone, without a furry companion, but then I met Howard, and he brought it up from time to time. A way to test the waters. First a dog, then a kid.

It wasn't too long after our initial one-night stand that we learned each other's full names. First and last. Howard Jacoby. That was how the sexual baseball metaphor went for us. First base—sex. Second base—learn each other's last name. Third base—meet the friend group.

I can't remember if we were sitting down for dinner or walking to the store or having a drink at Crush, but we talked about pets—the true sign of a committed relationship. Maybe it was only a conversation about having sex in front of a dog, not actually having one as a pet.

"I don't want to have a dog again," I'd said. "Their eyes are too emotive. How do people screw in front of them? You can tell exactly what a dog is thinking by looking at its eyes. Ugh. Imagine if he looked disappointed in you?"

We were both trying to cobble enough freelance writing work to look professional on our resumes and pay our rent. Back then, I cared that my name was listed in the byline of every article I wrote, but Howard only cared how much he was getting paid. He accepted any work that came his way: instruction manuals, flow-charts, proposals. I envied his lack of ego. He'd be a technical writer one week and a copywriter the next. He'd pen corporate newsletters or write goofy holiday mailers.

But I worked to develop my brand. My work was a reflection of me, and I was sleek and edgy and artistic. One could glean all of this from my social media accounts—my black and white headshot and noir background photo of an alley in Paris, or maybe it was Berlin.

We were talking about dogs. Howard pouted and brushed his bangs across his forehead. The face of a singer from an emo band. One mole under his left eye. An ever-present sadness. Ironically, Howard was never sad—at least he never showed it.

"You're disgusting," I said.

"I'm the grossest."

"I would never have sex with you in front of a dog," I said. "No pet for that matter."

"Not even a pug?"

"Especially not a pug."

Howard stood a few inches taller than me, a few pounds lighter. He talked and walked like he was from the Midwest, which he was. A heavy accent with an intentional gait.

If we were walking when we were talking about having sex in front of a dog, Howard would've stopped me, grabbed me, kissed me, but if we were at a bar, he would've held his tumbler of whiskey near his mouth without drinking, just warm sweet breath like fog over a pond. He was intoxicating back then.

Why can't I remember where we were?

I know he said, "They're a very, very powerful thing, a dog's eyes. You listen to any song written about a dog and you'd swear it was written about a lover."

"Is that your form of an aphrodisiac?"

"Is there any pet you actually would screw in front of?" Howard asked, holding my thigh tightly between his knees.

"A goldfish," I said. "Because their memories are only three seconds long."

"That's not true," Howard said. "It was a question at trivia last week."

"Would you?"

"Would I what?"

"Go home and screw?"

"I thought you'd never ask."

And that was what we did.

Sexual healing.

Chapter 6

I would never forget my first dog—Casey.

Decades ago. A blue tick hound with a hopeless stare and a gray muzzle from age, who followed me through my childhood home, watching a younger version of me dress in Fruit of the Loom underwear, Lee blue jeans, and a striped shirt before heading to the kitchen to pour a bowl of cold cereal to eat in front of the morning news. A researcher from the beginning. Casey stood at the front door as I left for school, and she waited for my return eight hours later.

Although my parents only owned a half-acre of land, our two-bedroom home in Perth, New York, built a century earlier, was surrounded by miles of rich soil with lush grass for haying and raising cattle and growing corn, but year by year the farmlands were sold, developed; and the sublime, yet underprivileged countryside transformed into everyman's suburbia. Two-story houses, swimming pools, white fences, and paved driveways. All this meant more people and more traffic. That was how Casey died—by the fruits of Capitalism.

A man around my father's age carried Casey from the road, across our meager plot of land, to our front door, where he kicked the frame with his muddy boot.

When I answered, he said, "Darted in front of me."

The scene didn't make any sense to my young mind.

"Casey?"

"I'm in a hurry," the man said, passing Casey from his arms into mine, and though I could barely hold her, my eight-year-old self didn't drop her.

The man hurried across the lawn, hopping into his pickup truck, and he drove off as quickly as he appeared. I remember the sticker on his tailgate. Years later I would learn that it was called an ichthys. Two intersecting arcs. The ends of the right side extending beyond the meeting point to resemble the profile of a fish.

I was only eight, and I'd accepted my first Communion. But for the first time in my life I thought, *What kind of God would kill without reason?* Casey brought no harm to the world; she was an old dog with a gray muzzle. But now she was dead, and the rest of the world wouldn't even notice.

When I told Mom and Dad, they looked at me suspiciously, chins to the side, weighing the truth of my story.

"So, this man just dropped the dog off and fled?" my father asked.

Dad worked as a union welder, his hands rough with calluses and tinged with everlasting grime. He talked as if I had something to hide—maybe he knew even before I did that I was holding onto a secret that would not reveal itself to me as a viable lifestyle until my senior year of college.

"What kind of car was it?" Dad asked.

"A truck," I said. "With a fish sticker."

"But what kind of truck? Ford, Chevy? Was it a Ranger or an S-10?"

"I don't know."

"You saw the fish sticker, but you can't tell me what truck it was?"

"He said he doesn't remember," Mom said.

Mom, I learned later in life, was not prepared to be a mother when I was born, instead yearning to go back to college to finish her bachelor's degree in nursing. But she wasn't one to branch out and follow her own path, if pressured against it.

"It doesn't add up," Dad repeated. "People don't just run

off. They fess up when they do something wrong. Didn't he leave his name?"

"I don't remember," I said.

"So, he could've left his name, but you don't remember. What do we even keep the notepad by the phone for if you're not going to write it down?"

"Maybe he's tired," Mom said. "Maybe he'll remember in the morning."

"That won't bring the dog back," he said. "She was a good dog."

"I'm sorry," I said.

"It's not your fault, sweet pea," Mom said.

"I just don't understand why someone would do that and leave," he continued. "It doesn't add up. He must've left his name. Maybe you just didn't write it down."

In bed, I cried myself to sleep, not because Casey was dead, but because my father didn't believe me. And while he was not always that cruel of a man, this I would never forget.

Chapter 7

The sky was a chameleon. After months of persistent Portland rain, the blanket of gray clouds was swapped out for white and blue camouflage. But that change didn't mean the end of rain because the moisture in the air still streaked the windows. The Pacific rains came and went like my moods. Growing up, I recognized these shifts. I couldn't tell you why, and I couldn't tell myself, "It's happening again." Every day I moved between a world of gloom and a world of glee.

A crow landed on the road and hopped to the sidewalk, pecking a bag of French fries, a half-eaten smash burger. The most excitement all week. I left the window, and I glared at my computer screen. How many hours a day did I stare blankly at this machine? When the pain developed behind my eyes, I knew it was time to end the workday.

That was life as a copywriter. One constant headache.

I wasn't always a writer. Once I was a teacher. But after I moved to Portland, I applied for jobs on Craigslist that required a master's degree, and I accepted the first offer. A contract writer for Google ads—sales descriptions for bicycle bells and vacation getaways to chalets in Arkansas—all to the tune of a dollar seventy-five above minimum wage. Six days later, my department was eliminated due to lack of funding. The official departure letter read "downsized".

Having Google on my resume boosted my worth on the job market, and it helped me land another job, and another, and suddenly I was juggling five freelance gigs. When the work was good, it was good; but the lulls in between made me question why I ever moved to Oregon.

When work ended, my headache wasn't like the usual headaches. There was heat with this one. Like a fire smoldering behind my eyes. It lasted through the night and the next morning.

When I couldn't look at the computer screen anymore, again, I wandered the apartment. Barefoot, treading the same path. Hardwood, but foot worn. Like a deer through the woods. I was aware of every detail. The places it creaked, the places it bowed. Aware of the walls. Where we nicked paint moving Howard's desk. Feeling the collective weight of the history of this object and that object—the chair, the couch, the wastebasket. Aware of our artwork, etched into my brain. How each piece cast its spell onto us. How each one told its own unique story from the time it was created. I often wondered if anything ever moved between the creator and the object. Could the painter pass along her illness through her paint brush? Infusing some life force into the work that over time bled out into our surroundings.

I used to be a khakis-and-button-up kind of guy, but at some point, I bought a leather bomber jacket believing it held the spirit I needed—a devil-may-care attitude—to give me the power from its years of legendary badassery. The leather bomber did not disappoint; it fortified me. And that was when I realized some objects have souls.

I paced and drank my coffee. I could've started another writing project, but instead I lifted my bare foot, pinched a small stone stuck between my toes. Where did this stone come from? California? El Salvador? Did it carry stories from that place?

The bottom of my foot was buttered with dust. Howard moved into the apartment four years ago, and some of the dust might've been from that time—from that man who was new to my life and in so many ways was my opposite. He'd never suggest we read some form of the *Kama Sutra* or implore we go skydiving. Stable and measured—two qualities I had desperately needed.

But now, I needed something new. Not traditional or expected. But spontaneous. Impulsive. In the past, that part of me—the reckless part—overwhelmed who I was, but I was older now. Didn't that also mean I could control myself?

The corners of the room and the crown molding and the details of our artwork, I knew it all. I looked at everything a hundred thousand million times. I was the god of this tiny domicile. But what had I missed?

I was obsessed by the creators of objects and their stories. Objects of permanence that would outlive their authors.

I finished my coffee, grounds like mud at the bottom of the mug. I sealed the top with my hand and turned it upside down, a chunk falling onto my palm. To me, it looked like a bleak future. But I wasn't a trained coffee reader.

I set the mug on the bathroom counter. Pissed so hard I'd have been embarrassed if I was in public. The bathroom smelled like rotten fruit.

Hanging above the toilet was a photograph. A reprint of the 1887 Eadweard Muybridge series I bought at the Portland Art Museum. Two half-naked boxers holding their fists to their chins. Across twelve frames, each boxer jabbed and hooked, bobbed and weaved. But that was not the most interesting thing about the photograph—that would be the photographer himself. Muybridge was a murderer. Two years after marrying a twenty-one-year-old named Flora Stone, Muybridge discovered that a drama critic, Major Harry Larkyns, was the true father of the couple's seven-month-old son. And Muybridge being Muybridge ventured from San Francisco to Calistoga, California, to track down the Major, eventually finding him in his cabin playing cribbage. Muybridge said, "Good evening, Major, my name is Muybridge, and here's the answer to the letter you sent my wife," then shot Major Harry Larkyns in the chest. In 1904, at his birthplace in England, Eadweard Muybridge would eventually die of prostate cancer. Given that he had shot a man to death, no one could say for certain that his cancer was not cosmic interplay.

Jiggling my penis in my jittery hand, I thought, *what did*

all of this add up to? The stories about everything we owned. But maybe that was it. Staring at the boxers as I zipped my fly, I thought, *maybe the photograph had bad energy. Could that be the cause of my terrible, unending headache?*

Late into the night, while Howard slept, I Googled real causes. It didn't take long to self-diagnose.

Yes, there were behavioral and emotional changes.

Impaired judgment—somewhat.

Inhibition—probably.

No impaired sense of smell or vision loss or paralysis on one side of the body. Not that I could tell. But I did have some memory loss—mostly related to drinking too much, too late.

It wasn't impossible to think that my search was wrong— that I didn't have a tumor in my frontal cortex. How I suddenly got cancer was the better question. But this I couldn't Google.

I didn't smoke or eat too much red meat. We didn't live beneath powerlines. Yet there was so much unknown that we brought into our home. The furniture and the dishware. The books and the artwork. I brought the Eadweard Muybridge photograph into this home, and he had cancer. Was the cancerous soul of the photograph festering inside of me now, leaping from object to species like some mutating virus? Because he had cancer and his photograph was on the wall, his entire history now emanated, pulsing like radioactive material. Seeping into everything. How could it not be from something in the house? Or was the photograph more like a cigarette? Something that needed a flame to cause cancer.

The artwork was in our home for this long, and neither of us had cancer headaches. But now Howard wasn't talking to me, and my head was on fire from the inside. Our neighbors were happy once, but now they weren't. Something was the cause of all this.

Everything on WebMD pointed to cancer, but I couldn't

say for certain. I needed a second opinion. I couldn't wait for an appointment; I had to see someone immediately.

I left the house as soon as I woke up, telling Howard I had to run an errand. At the ZoomCare office, I told the receptionist about my condition.

"Very, very sick," I said. "Cancer, I think. And the worst kind. In my brain."

Eighteen minutes later, I stood in front of a doctor.

I said, "It started with a headache. They're pretty common. But this one is different."

"Different?"

Dr. Kimberly looked almost identical to my father: the dark eyes and thin shoulders. Hands constructed for meticulous work. The way he questioned my story was something my father would do.

"Worse," I said. "It sounds weird, but I think it's environmental."

I wanted to tell him about the Eadweard Muybridge photograph.

"Do you live close to powerlines?" he asked.

"I live in an old doctor's office," I said. "Maybe there's something in the walls."

He said, "Have you been doing construction?"

"No," I said. "Nothing like that."

He told me my headache likely stemmed from too much computer time.

"Do you spend a lot of time reading on a monitor?"

"But that's not different than any other day," I argued.

He said, "Have there been any recent changes? Stress related?"

"Nothing really," I said. "My neighbors fight a lot. I can hear them."

"Have you thought about an eye exam?"

"As a cancer screening?"

"To help you read."

I didn't wear glasses, but I wasn't opposed to wearing glasses. Dr. Kimberly told me if I developed a cough, bloodshot eyes, or slurred speech, then I should come back.

"Try Advil," he said, as I was leaving.

"You don't believe me," I said.

"I believe the symptoms," he said. "Trust me. Advil. You'll be fine."

Something had caused the fire in my brain. But I walked to Walgreens for Advil and a pair of non-prescription glasses. $14.99 off the endcap. In thirty-minutes the headache disappeared.

Chapter 8

The Internet ruined hundreds of years of social patterns. Weekdays, weekends. What was the acceptable behavior for certain days of the week? Work wasn't just Monday through Friday.

On Saturday morning Howard sat at his desk finishing a project. White collar blues. His absence in bed destroyed any chance for us. His work required concentration, and I respected that; but I didn't agree with working on a weekend.

"Tonight's the storm," I said. "Are we doing something for it?"

Typing like the rhythm of the rain. The blue light of his screen swathed our room.

"Do you have to be so loud?" I asked.

My headache was back, and the glasses weren't helping. Didn't he care about my headache?

We spent all our time together, but did we really know each other? Maybe secrets were the key to a long, happy marriage. I had a few. I sat in bed watching him work, wondering what he would think if he knew my secrets.

Secret One: I was scared we'd drifted too far apart. I'd never shared this with Howard, because once you commit the words to sound, they become real. It was apparent we talked less, we fucked less, we shared less.

Secret Two: The depth of why I didn't want to become a father. How irresponsible it was for the environment. Overcrowding. The carbon footprint. And our sex life, it was already sputtering, and a child definitely wouldn't help. I could produce a stack of excuses too high to see over, if I ever let the conversation go on that long.

Secret Three: I'd always choose procrastination. "Idle hands are the devil's playground," my father said. For so long I thought he'd invented the phrase. But the superficial and fragile nature of life revealed itself to me in college. Reading the Russians, the Germans, the Existentialists. The first of my family to earn an advanced degree, I didn't want to follow in their footsteps. The way they complained about work and their miserable salaries and outrageous taxes. The never-ending daily loop of their lives. Wake, work, sleep, repeat. Simplifying the complexities of the world backed up my path to an English degree. Beginning with my dog Casey's hit-and-run and witnessing half the town being sold off, I was a convenient witness to an unkind humanity. Observing others was my superpower. That was the value of procrastination.

Howard left his desk, rummaging through the kitchen cupboards. I heard him fill the kettle with water.

"Will you bring back the peanut butter?" I yelled.

There was no answer. I used to sleepwalk and eat an entire jar when I was a child.

"Did you hear me?"

Howard's phone buzzed against his desk. He came back and looked at the screen to see who was calling. There he was—his beautifully dark emo hair, the teardrop birthmark below his eye, and that perfectly wide Midwestern nose.

"Did you bring the peanut butter?" I asked, but he held the phone to his ear.

Howard ignored me, listening intently. Then he moved toward the front door. I chased after him, but he held up his hand, one finger in the air. The gesture telling me to wait, don't come any closer, this is more important.

But what was more important than us?

Hand still in the air, he left the apartment. Was he disappearing right in front of me?

I watched him through the window. Wondered who he was talking to. Maybe his sister, or his mother, or an ex-lover.

Maybe he'd called the doctor about his aching hips. I knew he had secrets, too.

I opened the window to let in fresh air or hear bits of their conversation. I watched Howard back up between the buildings. With idle hands, I listened. But nothing. Only silence and the breeze and my thoughts.

Chapter 9

On the night of the twenty-first, several hours after sundown, the dark Portland sky was expected to erupt like a wildfire of streaking light. And animals were expected to wake, rattled from slumber, and make their animal noises. Birds chirping and squirrels chittering and dogs barking and cats meowing. All in a frenzied chorus.

We waited weeks for this event—a once every thirty-three and a half years' experience. The news was still split as to whether this was the end times or a celestial celebration.

We packed a beach bag with a bottle of red wine, salt and vinegar potato chips, and a blanket, joining hundreds of Portlanders in the park. Guitars and drum circles. The funk of marijuana in the air. It rained all morning, but by evening the sky was clear.

"I read that folks in other parts of the state are building fallout shelters. Stores supposedly are cleaned out," I said. "But here, it's just another reason to party. No one seems to care."

"I think it's political," Howard said. "How people react to the end of the world. What's it really matter what we do if we have no control?"

"What's it matter?" I asked. "This doesn't sound like you."

"Sorry," he said. "I'm just tired."

I thought about what he said. What if today was our last day together? What if the world as we knew it was truly going to end in the next few hours? I wandered around the apartment thinking of nothing else. Doom scrolling. Looking out the window. Would this be the last view I'd ever see? If historians could somehow read how I'd spent my last hours, they'd be shocked. Why didn't Thom do something special? Something meaningful? Why didn't Thom try to realize his fullest potential? But I was stuck. Maybe Howard was right. What did it matter? But instead, I dillydallied. Futzed about. Had that been what was upsetting him? I never even asked him how he was feeling today.

"What if it was?" I finally said.

"What if what was what?"

"Truly our last day together," I said. "Is this how you'd want to spend it?"

"Is this a trick question?" he asked. "I'd want to spend it with you, right?"

But he didn't sound convincing.

"Me too," I said. "But would you want to spend it with all these other people in a park? Or would we do something special?"

"Isn't this special?" he said. "But it's not like the world's really going to end. Nothing's going to happen. We're all just going to wake up tomorrow and go about our day like we do every single day."

"How do you know?"

"Because that's the world we live in. People blow everything out of proportion. That's just the way it is."

It was an argument I'd make. It felt like I was talking to myself.

"Do you really believe that?" I asked. I wasn't sure what I was asking him. I wasn't sure if I wanted to know if he thought everything was existential or that the Internet had shaped us to frenzy over news and then quickly forget about it. Why did he sound like me?

A woman raced up to our picnic. Her eyes were frenetic. Energy pulsing. Her long blonde hair swirling about as she bounced in place.

"Sky," I said. "I knew I was going to see you here."

"Diamonds," she said. "I hope you brought your diamonds. If this is as bad as they say it's going to be, diamonds can absorb the bad juju. You know that, right?"

"I remember you saying something like that once," I said. Sky had rented me the apartment. We were both young and naïve then, and she was my first friend in this new city.

"I think it's about to start. I love you two together. I love that we're all here together. Diamonds," she said, again, as she hurried away.

"I forgot our diamonds," Howard said.

"Don't make fun of her," I said. "She speaks from the heart, and I appreciate that."

"She's just a little woo-woo," Howard said.

A voice through a megaphone in the distance said, "Fear not what you do not understand." Followed by static and then silence.

"I wish we were more like that," I said. "She turns things into events. We never do that. If we'd brought diamonds, I don't think I'd ever forget tonight. Instead, we brought chips."

"I thought we'd just watch for a little while and not fight," Howard said, frustrated. "We don't even have diamonds."

"I'm not fighting," I said. "I'm just saying. Why can't I say things without you always responding?"

"Is this how you'd spend your last night on earth?" he asked, mocking me.

"Let's watch," I said. "You're right. I just want to watch in silence."

We'd been together for five years. We knew each other inside and out. And even events that happen once every thirty-three and a half years we can make seem like a Tuesday night eating leftovers. We were tired.

But at twelve nineteen, the first flicker of light buzzed the sky. If I didn't know better, I'd have thought it was a firefly shooting across my vision. Or phosphenes from pressing on my eyes too hard. But a few seconds later another spark streamed behind it. This one brighter, wider.

"Did you see that?" I said, grabbing Howard's hand.

I'd never seen anything like it. Flash after flash. After a few minutes the entire sky turned blue. Not quite like the daytime, but cerulean and green. It could pass for the Northern Lights. And hundreds of meteors—packs of a dozen or more—streamed side by side.

The crowd cheered around us. A festival of hope. The world wasn't going to end.

"It's unbelievable," I said.

"I've never," Howard said, trailing off. "In all my life."

"It makes you think there might be a god, doesn't it?"

"Shhh," he said. "I want to watch."

"This is how I'd spend it," I said. "My last night."

In a park with hundreds of others, we stared at the ethereal sky. Watching the Leonids, everything else seemed to vanish. The stress of our day. The paranoia that meteors would pummel the earth. The endless non-conversations about starting a family. All of it was gone. Distracted by something far out of our control.

Right now, it was just the two of us. And we were happy.

Deep-Sky Objects

Chapter 10

The soundtrack of firetrucks woke us.

Only hours after we went to bed, exhausted and exhilarated from a night of heaven's fireworks, sirens blared. And lights flashed. My mind was awake before my eyes, and I thought, *this is the end.*

I didn't expect it to happen like this. In a half-sleep in a warm bed. Alone in my thoughts. But then it dawned on me that this is exactly how I'd want it to happen. At peace.

But it was not the end of the world.

It was a fire at the warehouse across the street.

Howard made coffee while I watched the volunteer firefighters do what they did best, trying to save what was left of the warehouse. The sun had risen, and the new blue light spilled across the cityscape.

The choreographed procession of the firefighters' ballet mesmerized me. Racing with hoses as the boom of their ladder positioned itself perfectly. On cue. It was beautiful; it was exciting. The humdrum days of sitting at the computer writing had vanished. Two days of pure magic. But I was feverish for more. What was next?

All I could think about was how to add to this moment. Creating an experience. I needed diamonds.

I stood at the window, and then I knew what I had to do. I knew where to find my diamond moment.

Pulled to the window in our bedroom, I wanted to see what our neighbors—Kit and Lenni—were doing. Were they awake, absorbing the chaos of this morning? Their bedroom was still. Quiet. They must have been in their living room watching the firemen from their front window. It was a pastime of mine—watching people and seeing how they reacted to the events of their days. Their successes, their stressors.

The bedroom window was open, inviting—an early breeze blowing, smoke in the air. I could reach into their space if I tried. I thought how easy it would be to reach into their bedroom to steal something. This was not inconceivable because our window bordered theirs. A twelve-inch gap between buildings, and I could reach into their room, pick through their most secret possessions—the jar of women's hair removal gel on his side of the dresser or her bottle of men's cologne, Christian Dior Sauvage. In private, he sought her products and she enjoyed his.

I was grateful for the firefighters, breaking up my morning. But now I pondered stealing our neighbors' things. Everything is unprecedented, Howard had said. My brain had been rewritten by the last few years and the superlative nature of how we talked about everything.

Was this the best warehouse fire ever?

I needed more. But nothing too criminal. Just a small object, one the neighbors might never know went missing. That must be how it starts for people. First you accidently slip an object into your pocket, if for no other reason than to see if it would fit. Never actually serious about stealing it, because as soon as you put it in your pocket, you'd immediately take it out and put the bottle of Christian Dior Sauvage back onto her bureau. Or maybe you wouldn't. No, you'd take the bottle of Christian Dior Sauvage out of your pocket and you'd put it on your own bureau because you went through all that effort. Having to reach through your window, across the gap that separated your window from theirs. Think of how much effort that would take, and then ask yourself, if I went through so much effort, wasn't I deserving of that bottle of Christian Dior Sauvage? Truth be told, the neighbors were the sort of people who leave their blinds open daily and weren't troubled to raise their voices, no matter who was listening, while arguing over the tiniest infractions or namedropping well-connected friends or casually referencing the boutiques they bought all their belongings from. Certainly, it would be okay to take one small token from their home.

The firefighters had extinguished the blaze. They huddled in packs. Helmets off, jackets unzipped. Some of them drank Gatorade. They saved a warehouse. It was not the most glamorous story to tell their families when they got home that day. The world could've ended the night before, and today, they performed a routine job.

What did it all matter?

I stared into our neighbors' apartment. They owned much nicer furniture than we did—mid-century Danish. I know because I was home when the teak five-drawer dresser was delivered, and the Eames lounge chair and ottoman. But I couldn't count how many hours I saw their things unoccupied; an unused piece of furniture might as well be a standing tree or a grazing cow—contributing in some small way to the world. Did their things make their life more fulfilling? They couldn't, could they? So, didn't a couple who would leave their things to be cared for by no one deserve to have something stolen if it truly added no greater, gratifying joy to their life?

Watching their possessions from the interior of our bedroom—when the sun reached higher in the sky—three blocks of sunlight appeared to stretch across their chair and footrest. The most attention that chair experienced in a long, long time. I stood nose-to-glass, staring into their apartment, but the sun shifted, and suddenly the chair disappeared, and I saw my own reflection in their window. It was me, the same blue eyes of my childhood, except now I was a man about to steal a half-empty bottle of cologne from their dresser. And for what? So I could tell Howard? What was I supposed to say, "Hi honey, I stole from the neighbors. Isn't my life exciting? I created a memorable experience for myself, no diamonds needed."

I hardly recognized that man in the reflection, but I couldn't ignore the eyes. Those were all mine. Cerulean, like the color of the heavens the night before. Like the soul of God, my mother used to tell me.

As a child I had blonde hair, and I was rail thin, but then my blonde hair darkened, and my rail thinness turned into muscle in my college years, but then the muscle morphed into something closer to fat—not from lack of exercise, but curiosity, like when I saw an appetizer on a menu that I'd never tried, I tried it, and if an entrée included truffles, I tried that too, and when I couldn't pronounce a dessert, I'd one hundred percent order it—yet through it all, my eyes were always cerulean. The eyes of a pudgy thirty-five-year-old man and a rail thin boy. *That was me and this is also me*, I thought.

Howard drank his coffee and scrolled on his phone. I looked around our room—the same aesthetic since the day I moved in. I could suggest we needed a change, a trip to Ikea with six hundred dollars, and we could be new people with new things, but I didn't know what should be different. Our couch? The end table? Were we the type of people who would hang an oversized black and white screen-print of Audrey Hepburn on our wall? The world did not end, and that is what I cared about?

I stared into the neighbors' space and wondered if they cared about ours—if our furniture gave them anxiety. Did they feel a desperate need for some break in the monotony of the day? Is that why I felt like I wanted to race across the street to the smoldering ash of the warehouse, and find one still-hot coal, squeezing it into my palm, so I could have a scar, a reminder of this day—the day I did something spontaneous—something totally reckless—and then use that same coal to set fire to our apartment, too?

Did I want to burn down this life?

The night before I had a secret wish. Let something extraordinary happen. Something to reset our lives. To start all over. Maybe wake up as entirely different people. This was not the life I envisioned for myself.

I stared into the neighbors' space, through the blackberry vines that scaled the building and the thousands of prickles. One on their own couldn't hurt you, like one bad thought, but a thousand together could devastate you.

Chapter 11

I moved to Portland a decade earlier. During the spring of the Year of the Rat, I arrived and drove around the city with a property manager—Skylar Zigerowski. I met her at the first of two apartments, but as I waited in my car, I knew immediately that the first apartment wasn't for me. A chain link fence surrounded a two-story home. On the bottom floor, two black Labradors stood on the back of a couch and scratched aggressively at the window, frantically barking. I was waiting for them to break through the glass. Shards spraying across the yard. Something about the fierce, pent-up energy reminded me of my hometown.

Her Toyota pulled to the curb, and I waved from my window.

"Call me Sky," she said. "Like the sky. But my name."

"I hate to do this, but I don't think I need to see this one. Maybe we can go straight to the other one?"

"I wouldn't live in the Northeast either," Sky said. "Hop in."

Sky drove a gold Toyota Camry with a moonroof, and a dreamcatcher dangled from the rearview mirror. The interior smelled of sandalwood. She wore a blue crystal around her neck and told me of the neighborhoods. Young people lived in the Southeast section of the city, where we were heading, and older people lived in the Northeast.

She spoke with cocky sureness. "Yep, when you hit thirty, you turn in your Southeast residency card and head north of Burnside. But not a second sooner."

She told me there were six gay bars in the city: Cellar Bar, Eagle Bar, Embers, Red Cap Garage & Service Station, Scandals, and Escape Bar. Compared to my hometown—this was six times as many, which made Portland a wonderland.

Sky had majored in accounting, which was boring, so she

obtained her realtor's license.

"I thought about moving away, but there are too many cute girls in Portland," she said, winking at me.

"Your necklace is pretty," I said.

"Do you believe in crystals?"

"I grew up Catholic," I said. "I don't believe in anything anymore."

"It's larimar. My shaman says it's supposed to help me speak my emotions. Believe it or not, I used to be one of the shyest girls in high school. If you remember anything about today, remember that larimar is good and black opals are bad. It's important to know your stones. You can negate a black opal though by burying it with a diamond. My shaman knows everything."

"I've always heard larimar was a girl's best friend."

"Larimar and… never mind," Sky said. "I was going to say something really inappropriate."

"I thought you weren't shy."

"That's the problem with this thing. It's like someone opened a fire hydrant. Now every thought I have just spews out."

"I have the same problem," I confessed.

"A vibrator," she said.

I couldn't help but laugh. I liked her. The lack of a filter. There was something refreshing about her freedom, and I knew instantly we were going to be friends.

Sky instructed me I didn't want to live in Northwest Portland or the Pearl District unless I was originally from San Francisco or independently wealthy, and that yuppies lived in the Southwest, "But if big box stores are your thing, Beaverton is your place. Gag."

Driving past Colonel Summers Park, she pointed to the house of a musician.

"I loved Modest Mouse in college," I said. "Did you know they got their name from Virginia Woolf?"

"*A Room of One's Own* is like my *Bible*," Sky said, then she asked out of nowhere, "Do I seem like a witch? People say I seem like a witch."

"I don't get a witchy sense. But I don't know any witches."

"Sometimes when I talk about crystals, I think I sound a little woo-woo. But I'm not woo-woo, I swear."

"I don't mind a little woo-woo," I said.

"I like you," she said. "You have good energy."

She changed topics and said the park mostly catered to the homeless. Tents along the communal garden bordering the southern gate.

"It's really sad," she said. "The city doesn't help them at all, but the area dies down in the winter."

"Is he?" I asked, pointing at a guy on the sidewalk. Oil-matted hair under a Cape Cod bucket hat. A ragged coat over a flannel shirt. Ripped, greasy jeans, and he wore pieces of raw leather as shoes.

"That's a hipster," she said. "Trust fund kids think they're open-minded if they dress like that. That's the irony of this city. But if we followed him, he'd get into a Volvo, I swear."

"You should write a city guide," I said, and I meant it.

Sky parked in front of a brick building. Serviceberry shrubs and salmonberry bushes bloomed. Honey locust trees and dogwood trees bloomed. Even in spring, the grass was summer green.

I grew up in a place that possessed far fewer people per square mile, but here I could inhale and exhale with ease. My shoulders uncurled. This was where I belonged—and that feeling was entirely new.

"This could be your next home," Sky said. "The Dalai Lama says people are the masters of their own destiny." She rubbed the larimar hanging around her neck.

I never spent much energy contemplating destiny, but

I read enough about it in college. I remembered a course on Aristotle.

What is, necessarily is, when it is; and what is not, necessarily is not, when it is not.

I understood it to mean shit happens.

But maybe events were predetermined, and Skylar Zigerowski, the larimar-wearing witch, really did anticipate this course of my life—this exact apartment.

Maybe when Sky opened the door to the apartment to show me the old doctor's office, now updated with stainless steel appliances and mahogany cabinets, I had been thrust into a destiny that included Howard, and our neighbors Kit and Lenni, and the Leonids, and the burned warehouse, and everything down the line.

I scanned the apartment. It was cozy; it felt right.

"Do you love it?" she asked.

"Maybe it's fate."

The words echoed in the empty room.

Yet the sound traveled beyond the walls and the street, beyond Colonel Summers Park and the house where Isaac Brock lived, all six gay bars, and the shoreline of the Willamette River, where Portland grew from a shantytown to the hub that it is today—a place where people yearned to belong, where I knew I was meant to be.

Chapter 12

Blackberry bushes sprouted in the narrow gap between our apartment buildings. Year after year, they shot towards the sky, climbing with obsessive desperation. Vines encasing the entire side of the building only to be thrashed by day laborers. If they only knew how I watched them. Bored with my work and bored with the neighbors' apartment, I invented stories about the workers. The places they came from, the hardships they endured. Howard made fun of me for these regular fantasies. He said I needed coworkers.

Freelance writing is a modern-day disease, I thought. *Paid solitary confinement.*

The only time I couldn't see so easily into the neighbors' bedroom was late summer. That was when the berries ripened like fat black rubies and the crows and squirrels gorged until house cats lingered at the borderline. Those felines never negotiated the obstacle of thorny vines, but instead licked their stifles and waited for the squirrels to dawdle into the sunlight like drunks leaving a tavern after a liquid lunch.

By late summer, the cats had won. There were enough squirrel carcasses peppering the grounds that the landlord dragged his shovel along the dirt, because there was no sense balancing it across one shoulder; it would just plunge again to pry the next carcass from the earth. He dropped body after body into a black bag, and when the day was done—the grounds back to normal—he hefted the knotted plastic bag onto the bed of his pickup and drove off. How many bodies in the world leave the same way?

The day of the bramble removal, the temperature spiked. The record high for the month was set thirty-three years ago. Ninety-two degrees. But it was already one hundred and four when the workers showed up, swallowing their last sips of Gatorade.

No one had made any connection between the heat wave and the meteor showers, but I thought it was obvious. The prolific meteor showers occurred every thirty-three years, and it was thirty-three years ago when Portland saw its last heat wave.

But even on the hottest day in decades—eventually reaching one hundred and sixteen—a few insignificant, quiet drafts darted through the open window on the shady side of the building. This was how our neighbors, Kit and Lenni, left their apartment that day.

I stood at the bedroom window, staring again at her cologne bottle and his hair removal gel. All within arm's reach. Even with all the excitement of the last week, the firefighters and the warehouse fire, I wanted more. Always more. Some pinch of rebellion to contradict these humdrum days. I go back into my mind, thinking about my life. Was I always insatiable? I am a dog who can never get enough to eat. And I've had the thought more than once—after this life, I will be a hungry ghost.

The motors of weed whackers and hedge trimmers erupted—the irritating whine of engines eating through vines. Green spray against the workers' legs, their jeans forever chlorophyll stained. An hour of uninterrupted work eventually ended, and the men in leather gloves yanked the defeated strands of blackberry vines, dropping them to the earth without forgiveness. These sweat-laden men scattered and yelled and cackled and pointed at one another.

"Eres cobarde," they said.

The mayhem spooked the crows feasting on the juicy blackberries and they ejected themselves like clay targets from the remaining vines in a fluster of wing-beating chaos. But the squirrels could not escape so easily. Instead of racing down or leaping to their fate, the squirrels climbed higher, scurrying and hopping from vine to vine to reach the eaves. But one by one, they were pitched off as delirious men tore the trailers from their holds.

Except one squirrel. I remembered him. The perfect diamond on his chest. He was stout from a summer of feasting.

And street-smart, I thought, from foraging on fast food spilled by witching hour drunks, which was exactly why, when the particular vine he clung to was sawed in half and yanked to the ground, he dove into the nearest open window. And like a practiced action hero, he landed squarely on the expensive teak dresser, knocking the bottle of Dior from the ledge. But the squirrel wasn't afraid.

From the dresser he leaped onto the Eames chair, clinging to the leather. He surveyed the room and pawed his chin, chittered to himself, then stretched, puffing his chest—displaying his patch of fur. The diamond. He bent low, sniffed the leather, and scratched at the material. He dug a very small hole. I imagine what surprised him was the stuffing on the other side. The hole widened, and the squirrel yanked tiny gobs of puffy fabric.

For thirty minutes I watched the squirrel destroy the Eames chair and then the ottoman. The linen duvet and comforter next, followed by the pillows. He disappeared for another half hour, but I could picture all the mischief he would undertake.

Her underwear draped over the bedframe footboard torn to bits and then a pair of his boxer shorts. Maybe ransacking the kitchen and pantry of organic bananas and boxes of granola or chia seeds or at the very least a pile of dirty laundry behind the bathroom door. With the apartment in shambles, the squirrel returned to the window. But the workers had pulled down every last vine. The squirrel surveyed a landing, but he was too high from the ground to leap.

I imagined how this squirrel might die. It would not be a miscalculated jump to earth or a hungry cat or a speeding car, but an exterminator found on Craigslist. He would open their front door, shovel in hand, because he was a brutish killer. Unlike the landlord, who cleaned our grounds, this brutish killer was different because his tool was his instrument of death. A seasoned assassin, he would hunt the squirrel hiding for his life, maybe behind the bureau or a shoe stand, and the killer would thoughtlessly but reflexively whack the squirrel on top of the head. The blunt side of the shovel would certainly crush the squirrel's street-smart brain, as well as any final thoughts— memories of a squirrel brother, or the first time leaping from a tree, or racing around the trunk of a utility pole in chase of a lover—as the crisp memories vanished, fading like the sparks in his eyes before the killer scraped the lonely carcass from a polished wooden floor.

I emptied peanuts into my palm. Howard—who loved salted peanuts and stored this secret stash behind the olive oil in the cupboard above the stove—complained when I ate them. But this was different, I told myself, and opened our bedroom window, reaching into theirs and made an offering.

"Chk, chk, chk," I said. "It's okay, I'll take care of you."

Chapter 13

Who would let a squirrel die, if the answer to saving his life was so simple—a handful of salted peanuts?

There was a humble satisfaction in rescuing the squirrel from an almost certain demise. Buddhists believe that saving a life would increase their own lifespan, protect against illness, and remove obstacles from their path.

Howard believed that loving all living things was the noblest attribute man possessed. He did not kill on purpose. While he was your typical Midwestern Lutheran, he grew up living in a house in the Northern Highlands near Lake Superior, which had been blessed by a Buddhist monk. No mice or deer or insects were harmed in those great woods by him or his family. Everything lived. The daddy longlegs in his kitchen was captured by pint glass and freed on the front stoop, and the feverish mosquito landing on his forearm—as the sun lowered in the pink sky— would be cupped in his closed fist and shaken in the air, gently dizzying the tiny flying parasite. Like a child's game of "now you see me, now you don't."

Howard had told me, "It flies off, and you're forgotten. Like you shook that thought right out of its ear."

"Gone like you were never there at all," I said. "It's romantic."

"Like a goldfish," he'd said. "A three second memory."

"That's not true," I said.

"So, you do listen when I talk."

Even when Howard watched nature shows on TV, he got teary when apex predators—the lions of the plains—tore through lame antelope, or when African poachers shot down entire herds of elephants for their ivory or hunted gorillas for the meat or to make their parts into magical charms, chopping their furry hands off and using them for ashtrays sold in the derelict souvenir shops in the outskirts of Brazzaville.

In other words, Howard didn't prefer one animal to another but loved them all, which was why I enticed the chubby squirrel into our home. Howard told me stories from his youth when he charmed a raccoon into his house and kept it in his bedroom closet for two weeks, or when he cared for the rabbit his housecat Tinker Bell had maimed and left for dead. He was a good man, and I loved him for it.

The day the squirrel crashed into the neighbors' apartment, thrashing their furniture, our neighbor Lenni arrived home first. It was only apparent to me because of her exuberant shout that echoed through the open bedroom window into our home like a tidal wave.

"Who's the motherfucking kuningas?" she yelled.

The echo of the champagne cork popping followed by a pause. The ecstasy in her voice was heartening but equally heartbreaking. I knew what she would find when she opened her bedroom door.

When Kit and Lenni moved into their flat, without delay, they invited the entire neighborhood over for a housewarming party. It was a quiet, awkward affair despite the impressive variety of masquerade masks and bottles of Japanese whiskey Kit displayed on a rolling bar cart.

Kit worked as the creative director for an advertising firm downtown, and his claim to fame was a memorable e-commerce commercial starring a talking baby, who said, "Online trading made for people who probably know more than a baby, but then again, my stock portfolio's worth three-point-two million bucks." The commercial aired during the Super Bowl, and it catapulted Kit into advertising fame.

Lenni, however, taught watercolor painting at Oregon College of Art and Craft, where it was still possible to earn a degree in bookbinding, drawing, or the simple yet popular major—"Wood."

If you saw Lenni on the sidewalk in her oversized sunglasses it wouldn't be wrong to assume she was a model from Paris on vacation in the Pacific Northwest. Her dyed-blonde hair and cleft chin were characteristic of her ancestry, which I only knew about because she enjoyed slipping Finnish words, used correctly or not, into nearly every conversation, like when we first met at her housewarming party and she said, "Welcome to our kodikas home. Don't be afraid to drink too much. We have far too many leftovers from our last juhla."

Like Lenni, Kit had his own idiosyncrasies, although one might describe him as more of a dormant volcano, beautiful until erupting. He, too, could've walked straight from the pages of *Kinfolk* with his ruddy beard, flannel shirts, and cuffed denim jeans.

When Lenni's bedroom door finally opened, the champagne bottle hit the floor spewing like a geyser. From the darkened corner of our room, I watched through sliver-thin slats in the venetian blinds as Lenni moved in an anarchic pattern from one squirrel-destroyed item to the next, inspecting each piece but not saying a word.

I couldn't protect my childhood dog Casey, but a god somewhere in the universe was giving me a second chance to prove my worth. Those people with apricot pugs and adopted Syrian children better make a little room for me because I was joining their exclusive club of self-important caretakers.

I was an apex predator, but I was a savior too.

I said to our squirrel, "You're safe with me, sweet pea."

Never in my life would I be elected President of the United States, but on this day, I committed my first official pardon. The minor satisfaction left me feeling self-important. I thought, *I'm Thom, a real hero.*

I didn't wear a cape. I didn't need a mask. No sign around my neck. Let the squirrel see who saved his life, let him see the sincerity in my eyes as I saved him for his sake.

I had enticed the squirrel into our apartment; Howard would understand.

The plump squirrel's unaware behavior, nibbling bits of salted peanut from my outstretched palm, suggested a special misunderstanding about me. That humans (like the wolves and hammerhead sharks and polar bears who roamed the earth with violent sureness) weren't the world's deadliest apex predator. But the squirrel would be wrong.

I let him eat from my palm without crushing his fragile body, which would've only taken a couple seconds. One hundred and three pounds of pressure by the human hand. For such small bones, like his neck or skull, only a quarter of that would be needed. Computations of death, is that what this was? The researcher in me plotting every action. Realistic or not. Only to entertain myself.

But I wasn't that person—the killing type.

I said, "I'm five-nine, a hundred eighty pounds, and compared to a ten-foot polar bear, you should know that humans account for the deaths of a half million people a year, buddy. But I'm not like them. Instead, here I am feeding you. These hands, they could split an atom or destroy an entire nation. Did you know that?"

The squirrel looked at me for the first time. Tiny black eyes like smooth pebbles washed onto the shore. The squirrel didn't care what my hands could do, or not do, but what they did do, and in this moment, they fed him.

Chapter 14

The writer Henry David Thoreau said, "The squirrel you kill in jest, dies in earnest."

We named him Gordito. "Chubby" in Spanish.

From the moment Gordito leapt into my hands from Kit and Lenni's window—after methodically destroying their possessions—I knew he was always meant to find us. That feeling when something falls into place. You hear a click.

When Howard saw what I had done, he looked at me strangely. Gordito ran up my arm, burrowed into my shirt pocket, and poked his head out for a peanut while I scratched the diamond-shaped tuft on his chest. If Gordito could smile, he would.

"What do you think?" I said. "Can I keep him?"

"You're kidding, right?"

But he was the animal lover.

"He's the diamond I always wanted," I said. "I forget who told me, but diamonds protect people from evil. That's why we wear them as engagement rings."

"That's not true," Howard said. He had an encyclopedic mind. "The Ancient Egyptians thought there was a vein in your ring finger that went to the heart."

"Is there?"

"No."

"He's smarter than most humans," I told Gordito, who nodded. "Honey, he just nodded at me."

"Anthropomorphism," Howard said.

"Did you nod at me?" I asked, and Gordito nodded again.

"Howie, I'm serious."

Howard had always been the animal whisperer in our household, but on account of his pheromones, or because he reminded Gordito of some cruel human, when Howard knelt to offer Gordito a peanut, Gordito hissed. Standing on his hind legs, he postured like a cobra ready to strike.

It was immediately obvious that Gordito was smarter than most squirrels. Curious. Motivated by food. Trainable. While he posed like a prizefighter, I said, "Put up your dukes," and gave him a peanut.

He happily chomped it, and I held out another peanut, and said, "Put 'em up," and Gordito raised his tiny paws in the air.

"He's extraordinary," I said.

"He's probably somebody's pet," Howard said.

"I'm keeping him," I said.

Howard opened his laptop and began typing.

"What are you doing?"

"Googling why a squirrel for a pet is a really terrible idea."

"You've hounded me for years for a pet," I said.

"A dog," he said. "Or a cat. Definitely not a rodent."

I said, "If we send him back out there, you know what's going to happen to him."

But Howard was looking at his computer again. The glow of the screen on his face. He was absorbed.

"What is it?"

"I just got a news update," he said.

"About?"

Gordito stood on his hindlegs.

He opened another website. "They found it."

"Found what?"

"The size of a golf ball," Howard said. "It hit a power box. Look, there's a picture. Our apartment's in the background."

Howard held up his laptop. On the screen, a globular black mass, shiny and as smooth as silk. I had no idea what he was showing me.

"What is it?" I asked.

"The meteorite," he said. "It started the fire next door."

64

"A meteorite started the fire?"

"I can't believe it didn't burn up," he said.

"Jesus," I said. "Imagine if it hit one of us in the park."

"Now they think there might be more around the city," he said. "I was wondering why a crew was digging there all week."

I turned my attention to Gordito, staring into his black eyes. "Did you know about this?"

Gordito cocked his head, as if mulling the words in his brain. He looked at me, a soft stare, and his mouth began to tremble. Something brewing. Something miraculous about to happen. I could only imagine what he would say if he could talk. But his quivering lips settled, and he turned away, hurrying to the windowsill. Gordito gazed into the great big world.

What were you about to tell me, I wondered?

Chapter 15

Howard installed a sliding door in the window, and Gordito came and went as he pleased. Disappearing for hours but returning to our apartment when it was right for him, staying until he was rested and ready for the world again.

A housefly bumped against the glass. Round and thick and black. Over and over, knocking into the corner. If he was near the sliding door, I would free him into the world. But he continued working his body against the glass like it was on purpose.

When Gordito was gone, Howard and I would go about our day. Working. Cleaning. Laundry. I imagined what he must've been doing. How does a squirrel spend his day? It felt like a foolish thing to talk about with Howard. I slid the door in the window open anyway, staring into the world. All the possibility. But the housefly didn't react. Tossing himself at the same spot. Waiting for one or the other to give.

"Ground control to Major Thom," Howard said.

"Huh?"

"I was asking you something," he said. "What about the pet clause in the lease?"

"What clause?" I said, smirking. I was the apex predator. Able to kill or save. And I would save Gordito because I was one of the good ones.

"That's not what you used to say."

"It's the *right* thing to do," I said. "And we need to spice things up."

"It's the thing *you* want to do."

"What does that mean?"

"You get obsessed," Howard said.

For years we've been doing the same thing over and over

again. Our relationship was a lifeless task. I needed something to look forward to.

"Maybe," I said, agreeing with him.

I just needed more.

The housefly bashed and bashed and bashed. I raised my arm, slowly. Hand circling the air with the housefly's movement. I'd trap him beneath my palm, his vehicle to safety.

"Hey," I said, as I concentrated. "Did you hear the one about catching a polar bear?"

"Is this a joke?"

"You cut a hole in the ice," I said, the words flowing without feeling. "And you put some green peas around the edge, and when the bear comes to take a pea…"

"I don't know if you're being serious, or if you're being funny," Howard said.

"When the bear comes to take a pea," I repeated, more strongly. "You kick him in the icehole."

Striking my hand forward, I cupped the housefly against the glass. The suddenness caught him off guard, and his wings buzzed. Fierce and frantic.

"You seem like you're in a daze," Howard said. "Should I be worrying about you?"

"I'm… fine," I said.

Was this better or worse for him?

We've been doing the same thing over and over and over and over and over and over and over. Our relationship was a task. What was I looking forward to? Buzzing and buzzing and buzzing and buzzing. Poor thing. Trapped and scared, and if I let him go, he'd only go back to that dark, dark place. Throwing himself at The Meaningless Something, until his body couldn't take it. A long, slow attempt at splitting himself in half.

Howard said, "Did you hear me?"

"Huh?" I said, again.

"Sometimes it seems like you're not even paying attention."

"There, there," I said, flattening my hand against the glass, as the buzzing ended.

Chapter 16

Howard collected Snapple caps. He insisted the facts printed on them helped him at trivia night. He'd reach into a Quaker Oats canister brimming with caps under his nightstand, reading a few before bed, always impersonating Keanu Reeves. He read the facts for himself but changed his voice for me. Humor makes strange habits more digestible, I'd told him once. I think he'd caught me in the middle of the night finishing another jar of peanut butter, so I squealed like a pig.

But Gordito found another use for his Snapple caps. Fetch. He never tired of fetch, no matter how many times I tossed a cap into the corner of the room. Skipping the cap across the floor, Gordito always snatched it before it stopped.

Tonight, as we finished work, Gordito cozied himself in his shoebox. Howard saved his last work document on his computer, and I thumbed the safety button on a Snapple cap.

Thwop.

The noise thrilled Gordito, who darted from his box.

I gave the cap a double-*thwop*, and Gordito raced back and forth.

"Ready, boy?"

I bounced the cap off two walls, and Gordito sped after it like a greyhound. The double-click even got Howard's attention, who said, "Bring it to me, please."

But Gordito did not. I reached into my sweatpants pocket and fed him a peanut.

Howard eyed him sideways. A look that said, "Traitor."

"What makes you think he'd bring it to you?" I asked.

"Loyalty," Howard said. "Do it again. But do it with the lights off so he doesn't know who throws it."

I pointed towards the light switch.

"You, and I'll throw," I said.

Howard groaned as he stood from his desk, but he hobbled to the light switch. The color of things changed from blue to gray and black.

In the dark, I said. "What do you bet he brings it to me?"

"He won't," Howard called back.

Maybe it was the darkness that made me feel brave. "A blowie?" I asked.

I knew it wasn't sexy to ask for it, and I wasn't trying to get into a fight.

"Then what do I get?"

A *kid*, is what came to mind. A cruel thought to think; but quick thought come, quick thought go. I had a terrible filter. But there were some things I could never joke about. So, I said, "Forget it."

Howard, though, said, "Are you gonna throw it, or not?"

I pitched the cap across the floor. The pitter-patter of tiny nails clicking with distinction. Tap, tap, tappity-tap, tappity-tap, tappity-tap, tappity-tappity-tap. Out and back. And then I felt the tug of his nails on my sweats as he climbed my leg, burrowing into my pocket for another peanut.

Howard flipped on the light switch, the room instantly aglow, but Gordito had disappeared. Howard looked around the room. But I shrugged. Howard knelt on the floor, scanning under the bed.

Gordito squirmed inside my pocket, nibbling a peanut, but I tugged my shirt over him.

Howard crawled towards me. At first with curiosity for Gordito, and then it dawned on him that he was on all fours. He moved knowing that I was watching him. Slowing his movements, locking eyes with me briefly, then looking away. He craned his neck, so I could see his profile, and he jutted his tongue into his cheek. A bulge growing.

He wagged his finger at me.

"Tease," I said.

Howard scooted across the floor and sat heavily beside Gordito's shoebox.

"If he's inside," Howard said. "No one wins."

We had these moments when I wasn't overthinking what he was thinking. I imagined Gordito chasing another squirrel around a utility pole. Life could sometimes be easy. Howard lifted the lid of the shoebox.

"Ready for a fact?" I said, holding up the Snapple cap, as Gordito crawled out of my pocket. I can't remember another cap I'd ever read to him.

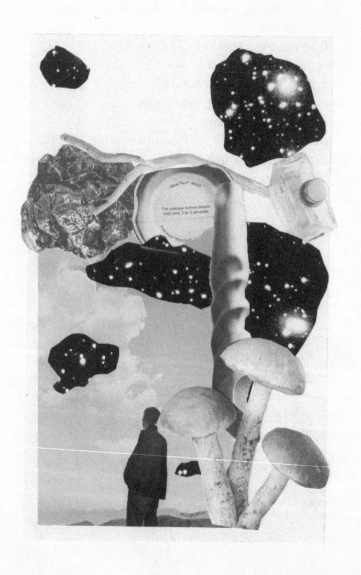

Chapter 17

"Fish cough."

Chapter 18

Once a quieter home, Kit and Lenni now fought with fierce intensity. Their relationship was ruptured—a weak spot hammered until it burst wide open. Did they experience that breakdown buying new things to replace what Gordito destroyed? The yelling, the crying, the palpable silence in between. None of it could be escaped.

With their window open, it was impossible not to hear them.

"Did you see the news today?" Kit asked.

"I don't want to know what's going on in the world," Lenni said. "Huonot uutiset. Do you know what I'm saying? It's all bad news."

"I can't believe it." Kit steamrolled her anyways. "The whole government. It's, what's the word, perverse."

Lenni said, "Are you trying to get into a fight? Because if you're trying to get into a fight, you're going to lose."

"By telling you the news, Len? You're going to hear about it one way or another. It's the news. It'll find you."

"You're kidding me," Lenni struck back. Her voice changing. The words slowing. "I had no idea how that worked. And here I am thinking I was different. What's the word for what you are? Dickhead."

"Calm down," he said. "I was saying it metaphorically."

She let out an earsplitting scream. I couldn't see her, but I could imagine the pterodactyl wings bursting from her shoulder blades—knocking over the lamps and sweeping the coasters to the floor—as they stretched to the walls. Her neck extending until her head hit the ceiling. Face covered in scaley green flesh, jaw a horny beak with rows and rows of needle-sharp teeth. Lenni the wild beast. It was that type of scream.

And then there was Kit—a meal of soft flesh in a tin bucket. I couldn't listen to her eviscerate him, again.

But like a volcano he would wait until suddenly he would say the thing he always said, the thing that would send her fleeing, locking herself in the bathroom.

"Well, if you could have a kid maybe things between us would be different."

I grabbed a tennis ball, and Gordito followed me to the sidewalk. I pitched the ball against the building. A lonesome act from my childhood. I could see my younger self, and I could see myself old and gray, both versions retreating to some abandoned space to calm my nerves and play catch. The release of energy with each throw and the satisfaction of the retrieval. It was a perfect game.

The lot across the street had been cleared of debris, but some heavy equipment remained. Once a warehouse, now an investigation site. Yellow tape to keep people out frayed and blew untethered with the breeze. During the week, an unmarked car pulled to the scene, and a few professional-looking individuals in suits would exit the car for a few minutes, point their fingers around the lot, and then get back into the car and drive off. But today, the site was unpatrolled.

It would never be a famous site. There was no giant meteorite the size of a Volkswagen. Instead, a stone—smaller than a fist—was found stuck in the trunk of an oak tree. A stray that had wandered from the pack during the Leonids. I knew how it must've felt. Being so alone and thinking the only way to save yourself was to escape. Wasn't that why I moved to Portland in the first place?

On its return, the tennis ball stubbed my ring finger, ricocheting across the road. Gordito raced after it, as I yelled for him to stop.

A pile of junk had been left on the corner. I made a quick mental note: Call the Bureau of Environmental Services. Their number saved in my phone. Every week, people moved away from Portland. As rent increased in leaps and bounds, the working class fled. It was only a matter of time before Howard and I left our own piles of junk on the sidewalk. Some sad reminder that we were once here. Broken chairs or clay pots. Spare tires or bookshelves. But working-class city workers always came to the rescue. Sweeping every last bit away—because in so many ways a clean city was a problem-free city. We are the snake that eats itself.

As Gordito crossed the road, I screamed for him.

"Watch out for cars." The terror of losing my dog Casey all over again.

But Gordito grasped the tennis ball in both paws.

In the middle of the warehouse lot, he stood on his hind legs.

A boy—maybe ten or twelve—riding his bicycle stopped.

"Is that for real?" the boy asked.

"Is anything real?" I joked. I didn't mean anything by it. Just thoughts sliding into being without a filter.

"Make him do it again," the boy commanded.

I held out a peanut for Gordito.

"Bring it back, buddy," I said. But Gordito remained unsure of his audience.

The boy said, "Is he going to do it or not?"

"Come on, Gordy."

One step and then another. Gordito walked with the caution of a toddler, swaying as he waddled forward. He dropped the tennis ball at my feet.

The boy let go of his bicycle, and along the side of the street, he scooped a handful of pebbles.

"Have him fetch these," he said, hurling the stones at us.

"What the hell's wrong with you, you little fucker!"

Gordito fled to the lone tree on the lot. A place of safety even though half the tree was burned black from the fire.

I didn't have much experience with children.

"Are you an idiot?" I asked.

"I didn't mean it," the boy said, lowering his eyes.

He didn't know how to avoid predation—some creative or interesting way to outsmart a more cunning animal. When would he learn that skill? The impulse to act first was always present. In all fairness, I was just as impulsive. But I was bigger.

"Go home," I said. "Before you get into more trouble."

"No," he said. "I have ten more minutes."

I held out my phone like a warning, and then I said, "I'll call the cops."

The boy hurried away.

Gordito perched high in the half-charred oak tree. Maybe this was how our relationship would end. Looking at one another from different heights. It was something Howard and I could tell our friends in the future. "We had a pet squirrel once."

But hearing my voice, he descended.

"You ready for a cocktail?" I asked.

He toddled forward, but he wasn't bringing me the tennis ball. It was a shiny black stone, as round and smooth as a pebble from the sea. When I reached for the stone, I noticed thin white veins striating the surface. Unlike any stone I knew. But incredibly familiar.

I've seen this before, I thought.

"What is it?" I asked, the words as automatic as my breath.

I watched Gordito's mouth begin to open. Squirrels can vocalize, mostly squeaks and chirps; but the way his lips moved I knew he was about to say words. English words.

There was no one around who could confirm what was happening, yet I heard it with my own two ears.

"It's part of the meteorite," I heard. I wasn't making it up.

Gordito's black eyes looked like plump fruit seeds. He stood on his hind legs, arms raised, holding the small stone—the fragment of the meteorite—like it was an offering, and I was some mythical god.

I took the stone from him. The weight was significant for something so small.

Gordito continued to hold his arms in the air. I saw feeling in his eyes and gave him another peanut. He wedged it deep in the corner of his cheek. Then he raced back across the street, towards the rear of our building, towards our entrance.

I stood alone for a few moments. The empty lot. The yellow caution tape. The half-charred oak tree. And the weight of something far greater than a stone in my hand. I turned the tiny meteorite fragment over and over with my fingers. The weight pressed into my fingerprints, as if something within the stone was pushing back against me.

"What am I supposed to do with you?"

Chapter 19

There was a pattern to Gordito's days. Seven to ten in the morning he foraged, took a siesta at noon, and abandoned us at sunset. Throughout the year, we watched his chubby body vanish into a svelte version. And while his body transformed, so too did Howard's.

He closed the bathroom door with the fan still running when I first noticed it.

"Howard, your mouth," I said. "Are you okay?"

His lower lip sagged heavily to one side.

I said, "Did you hurt yourself?"

He returned to the bathroom and looked at himself in the mirror. "Bit … lip."

"Honey, it looks real bad."

First his aching hips and erectile dysfunction, both taking their toll. He wouldn't do anything about those problems. The stubbornness led to more nagging, which led to more tension, which amounted to longer stretches of silence. It was almost like his mouth had slowly vanished from lack of use. I blamed his Midwestern-ness for his inability to talk about his feelings, and he pointed to my passive aggressive nature.

I hadn't told him about the meteorite. I hid the alien fragment on my nightstand, in a decorative dish among memorial objects of our past. A glittery peach sunstone found on a hike at Mount Hood, an Anadara fossil from the Oregon coast, a buffalo nickel, some spare change from Turkey, and the meteorite— black and polished by space.

"Howie, you really need to go to the doctor."

But he never did.

The next day Howard's appearance continued to change. The swollen lip spread to the entire side of his face. Mouth tilted, cheek sagging. Even his left eye looked tired, half-shut.

"Howie, I mean it, you really need to go to the doctor."

On the third day, he said he wasn't going to work.

"Howie, please, you really need to go to the doctor."

"No work," he said, like his mouth was full of marbles. "Screen hurts."

"If it's that bad," I said, "you have to see somebody."

It was like I was a child's toy. Pull my cord and I only say, "Go to the doctor."

"Sleep now," he said, going to bed.

In the corner of our room, we had an armchair—a linen seersucker inherited from Howard's grandmother, and on that linen seersucker armchair, we set a birdhouse, new from Bi-Mart. It was an upgrade from the shoebox Gordito previously called home.

Howard wasn't working, per se, but was still doing his chores. Cleaning Gordito's birdhouse, refilling his seed bowl. It seemed like the only thing that was still making him happy.

"He's really getting skinny," I said to Howard, as he put down fresh newspaper. "I hope he's not sick. Or we'll have to bring him to the vet. If he keeps getting skinnier, don't you think we should take him to a specialist?"

I couldn't say if Howard was ignoring me, or if he didn't hear me, and if he didn't hear me, were his ears next?

We moved around one another like ghosts—tiptoeing around the obvious.

"I Googled some things," I continued. "Have you ever heard of Bell's Palsy?"

Howard never reacted, no matter what I said. Instead, he went about his business. Getting up, eating breakfast, going back to bed.

"I don't understand what's happening," I said. "Why won't you talk to me?"

"What say?" he asked.

But I didn't understand.

"Your mouth," I said.

"Hurt," he interrupted me.

"Your mouth hurts?" I asked. "Is that all?"

"Hurt," he repeated.

Howard and Gordito were developing their bond as we lost ours. Howard spent nearly all his time caring for Gordito, and Gordito wouldn't let Howard leave his sight. If Howard left the room, Gordito followed. If he went outside, Gordito raced to the window. If Howard shut the bathroom door, Gordito scurried back and forth across the base, scratching to burrow underneath.

"When's the last time you worked?" I asked Howard.

His eye nearly closed, his lip hanging lower. Maybe a stranger wouldn't notice the change, but I did.

"Are you depressed?" I asked. "Is that it?"

The hollow echo of my own words.

When I first saw the apartment with Sky, the space was filled with so much hope. What was left?

Chapter 20

In the space between buildings—where menacing blackberry bushes flourished and Gordito had leapt from impending death into our home—Armin, the landlord, promised us that by planting tomato seeds, they would usurp the invasive vines. A trick from the old country, his words.

Change was happening everywhere. Around Portland, the increasing population of houseless people rivaled the number of new apartment buildings. How I envied the gods who didn't worry themselves with the absolutes but could appreciate the all-togetherness of opposites existing at once.

Howard was falling apart before my eyes, and Gordito the passive became Gordito the predator, who came home with the corpse of a baby flycatcher, the size of a half dollar. The kill dropped onto our wooden floor. Gordito rubbed his paws, chattering, springing from one side of the bird to the other in a wild celebration of death. When Howard tried to scoop the bird, Gordito snarled, lunging to bite.

Howard glared. He could barely say the words, his mouth moving awkwardly.

"What … you?"

"Let me try," I said, but Gordito stood on his hind legs, ready to fight.

Howard grunted and circled Gordito, who watched his every move. Eventually he calmed and retreated to his birdhouse on the armchair, leaving his kill in peace.

I wrapped the dead flycatcher in a paper towel, and said, "What's gotten into him?"

Howard shook his head. His eye was entirely closed, and he brushed at it with the back of his hand like a cat.

"Are you okay?"

But he said nothing.

Craig Buchner

I double wrapped the bird in a plastic shopping bag and carried it to the dumpster. Outside, I looked at the sky. What was happening beyond our atmosphere? Meteor showers. Radiation moving within light. Dead planets and budding stars. All within a vast black vacuum. So much, and I was all the way down here holding a dead bird.

When I returned, Howard was sitting on the bed. Gordito ate birdseed from his palm.

"You guys made up," I said.

Howard nodded.

"Can we talk?"

He nodded again.

"What's bothering you?" I said. "These last few, well, it can't keep going on like this, right?"

"Father ... hood," Howard said.

"Fatherhood?" I asked. "You're Gordito's father."

Howard patted his chest.

"I know," I said. "You're amazing. I just don't know about me."

Howard looked straight at me with his one good eye. Unblinking. He had planned a trip to Wisconsin to visit his sister's newborn son. Howard was an uncle two times over. He was leaving the next day.

"You mean us?" I asked.

"Us," he repeated.

The two of us becoming three.

"I'm trying to get there," I said. "You won't believe me, but I read an article online. Ten ways to be an amazing parent with your spouse. Number six on the list was—I kid you not—you should at least still be talking to each other."

Howard laughed. I'd forgotten what it sounded like. Not his laugh, per se, but getting along.

"They say you're never truly ready," I said.

83

He motioned me forward. I sat on his lap, and he put his arm around me. I kissed the sweet spot on his neck. It was different from how Antonio kissed me.

"Keep … talking," he said.

"When you get back," I said. "I promise I won't shut down."

Without him, Gordito rarely left his birdhouse except for when Howard called on Skype. I told him everything I could think of to keep the conversation going. It had been so long since we connected, I didn't want it to end. I told him what I ate for breakfast, what time Gordito woke up, what Snapple caps I tossed for fetch.

Gordito raced around the room searching for Howard. I pointed at the computer screen, but the digital version was not enough.

During those days alone, Gordito and I kept to ourselves. Alone with my thoughts, I couldn't help but wonder what I'd do without Howard. I sat at the edge of the bed, holding the meteorite, thinking of another life. The rock was heavier than the last time. Not bigger. But twice as heavy.

The meteorite was a stranger in a strange land, and of all the people to meet, it was here—in my hand. My mind wandered. An introduction was in order.

"I'm Thom," I said. "Nice to meet you."

Of course, there was no response.

"I'm an apex predator," I said to this thing from outer space. "What's it like where you came from?"

Imagining the jolts of lightning coursing through the atmosphere and meteorites crashing through the clouds. A barren landscape of rocks and dust. The atmosphere swelling with heat-trapping gases. Mysterious beings hidden in the soil and swimming in subsurface rivers. The rock began to warm in my hand.

"What on earth?"

My palm tingled. Like my hand had fallen asleep. Not from the heat of my skin but the inside of the rock. I rubbed my thumb against it, but the surface was suddenly, strangely cool now. How was it both cool and warm? I thought about the Eadweard Muybridge painting and my headache. How I'd convinced myself that a painting could infect our house. I knew it sounded crazy, but what if I'd invited an intruder into our home, again? What did I really know about the meteorite?

As soon as Howard returned—a midnight flight into Portland—he made his way straight into bed. Gordito followed, hurrying onto his pillow. Howard trembled, and I rubbed his neck.

"God, you're freezing," I said.

He breathed quickly, while I made him a cup of ginger tea.

"Was the baby sick?"

He shook his head.

"You should sleep," I said, and turned out the lights. I kissed his forehead. "I'll sleep on the couch."

Howard rarely got sick. I couldn't imagine what it would be like if it was serious.

Gordito and Howard slept, and I walked around the neighborhood. Portland at night was calm. No traffic or voices. Just the lush trees silently growing. A world of life invisible to the naked eye. Our neighbors and the squirrels without worry of crime or violence or sickness. I'm sure Howard was fine. He would feel better in the morning.

I thought of walking to Crush. Meeting a man. Letting him fuck me in the bathroom. But we were talking about starting a family. That was not *us* anymore.

Blue spruce

Picea pungens has the small, thin, pointed needles typical of the spruce family. This cone-bearing tree may be 100 feet or more tall. It is used as a garden tree.

Chapter 21

December 18, the 352nd day of the year—thirteen days until the New Year.

We watched *The Babadook*—a horror movie. I couldn't lay my head across Howard's chest. Not like before. Not like when we were younger, when laying that close would lead to sex.

There was something different about him. Beyond the silence, beyond the one shut eye, he was a different person. His hair was thinner, the skin around his temples pushing further and further back. More and more of him disappearing. Us disappearing.

I watched him watch the movie. One pupil darting around the screen. What was he looking at? What did he see through that one good eye?

I wondered if the movie was watching us back; what would it see? Would it be bored? Two men a foot apart. Motionless. Passive. But what if the Babadook saw me reach between Howard's legs and grab his dick?

Howard shifted his hips away, and after a few seconds, I said, "What's wrong? Are you mad at me?"

Howard moved back. One eye like a cyclops.

"Tired," he said.

"I know it'll feel forced, but let me try."

I spit on my palm, gripping his penis with my thumb and forefinger, pumping the soft flesh a dozen tries.

But nothing.

"Touch … you," he said, guiding my hand between my own legs.

The movie was ending. The character Amelia finally acknowledged the Babadook—the monster—as a permanent presence. Like our lack of communication.

Is this the way it's always going to be? Two steps forward,

one step back. The monster always present.

He kissed my forehead, then rolled away. I did the same and closed my eyes. The liberty pose—but there was no freedom. No. We were prisoners.

I dreamed of my father standing in the corner of the room watching us. It was not a dream about black cats or souls. The room began to smoke. Smoke from the floorboards, smoke from the walls, smoke blurring my sight. I could hear him—his soothing wordless hum. Even in the smoke. Even in the dark. The sounds became words.

"In the event of a decompression, Thommy, an oxygen mask will automatically appear in front of you. Place it firmly over your nose and mouth, son. Secure the elastic band behind your head, and breathe normally," my father in my dream said. "If you're traveling with a child who requires assistance, secure your mask on first, son. Secure your mask first. Your mask first. Your mask first. You first, son. You first, son. Your first son. Your first son. Your first son."

Chanting until I was enchanted.

But like a needle scratching across vinyl, a terrible screech in the real world jarred me from this sleep and hurled me into consciousness.

Gordito darted out of his birdhouse, nails digging into the venetian blind as he raced up the wall.

As I swam out of that dream, it was difficult to tell where I was. In this life or on some other planet. Howard turned on the bedside lamp, and Gordito shrieked with wild terror as a coiling black monster hunted him.

We had fallen asleep watching a horror movie about a beast that sneaks into your home through a child's book, but this was no film. The bony creature was in our room. Right now.

As the sleep washed away, I could see clearly.

A black ferret.

Howard whipped the comforter from his body, reaching for Gordito's empty birdhouse. In two steps he rounded the bed, pitching the structure at the ferret. A wallop against the wall, followed by shouting at the front door of our apartment.

So much noise and violence.

But even with one eye, Howard moved like a trained killer. The ferret fell from the wall, regaining composure, and set its sights on Gordito again. The ferret's eyes black like the meteorite. Shiny and streaked with glowing white veins. An animal possessed. Howard lurched, seizing the ferret by the center of its body, and the animal coiled around his arm like a serpent. Biting into his flesh. A swatch of blood on his forearm.

Howard slammed the beast against the wall. Uncoiled now, it fought back. Flailing, flopping. Teeth like needles and red, red blood. The sound of actual wildness. It took a moment to remember the beginning: before walls, and computers, and tools, and medicine, and farming, back to our basic survival instincts. The impulsivity of cavemen in a wild, strange world.

Howard punched the ferret in the center of its mass and threw it to the floor. He stomped at the animal. I hoped he would split its head with his heel, but it darted between his feet.

The pounding at the door continued.

"Is Tracy in there?" a voice yelled. "Don't hurt her."

Tracy, the ferret, had vanished. Howard tucked Gordito into the small birdhouse, the roof nearly destroyed. He handed it off to me, before he resumed his own hunt.

Again, the pounding.

Howard opened the door. Later we learned his name was Blaze—our new neighbor.

"Where is she? She's only a jill."

Denim shorts, bare chest, arms tattooed with koi. He wagged an eighteen-inch strip of beef jerky and crawled around the floor.

"Tracy want a nibbles?"

"It's possessed," I said. "You can see that, can't you?"

Blaze said, "These animals aren't going to hurt you, honey."

He crept into our bedroom, then stopped. He made a snickering noise, like a rodent. Then reaching under the bed, he yanked the stealthy ferret from the darkness.

"Here we are, sugar."

Blaze fed Tracy the beef jerky, and she relaxed in his arms.

"He's fucking bleeding," I said, Howard's arm on display for Blaze, now sitting Indian style on our bedroom floor with a ferret gnawing the meat.

Even Howard, who to all appearances had such a mellow composure, born under the sign Libra, could not restrain his energy—shaking so hard I thought he was going to rupture.

"That thing's dangerous," I said.

Blaze corrected me. "Tracy."

Howard was a bear trap ready to spring. Shoulders drawn back, fists clenched.

"It tried to kill our squirrel."

"Squirrel?" Blaze said. "They're not domesticated."

Howard had been bitten three times. Inside his wrist, on his ring finger, and on his bicep.

Blaze said, "I'm guessing yours isn't a service animal."

"Get the fuck out," I said.

Blaze held the prying animal who was scanning for Gordito—the hunt still on.

"Shush, honey bear. We're going home now."

When they were gone, we opened the birdhouse, peeling the roof away completely, to find Gordito backed into the corner. He was an impressive creature. What did it feel like to be stalked, considered food or simply something to kill to remedy boredom? Howard and I had once known a form of lust that at times we joked was animalistic. One of us the predator, the other

90

prey, but fueled by a different kind of hunger.

In the silence of our apartment, it was easy to imagine what would've happened if Howard had not intervened. If the worst had happened.

Gordito would be dead. I would be crying. Howard would punch a hole in the wall. The ferret might also be dead. Blaze might have a black eye or a broken jaw or he might be dead. Howard would be arrested. We would be evicted.

In life, there was always *if*. If this, if that. If then, if, if, if.

But this was now, and this was us.

In a matter of minutes, Gordito no longer trembled, and he spied out of the peephole, sniffing the air. He chittered and ran onto the comforter, first scratching at the blanket, then curling into a ball.

Howard looked at me.

"Are you okay?"

He nodded.

"He thinks we're his family," I said. "It's up to us to protect him."

"You make," he said, "good dad."

I stared at him blankly. Not with disinterest or without emotion. But trying to understand how that made me feel.

Howard held my hand, rubbing his thumb across my knuckles, and I squeezed his hand three times. Three simple words.

I.

Love.

You.

Chapter 22

The Pacific rain stopped for a week and months of clouds guarding the sky like a gray cocoon folded back on themselves to reveal a cobalt heaven.

I opened each window, and the wind blew the scent of winter daphne and purple saucer magnolias into our home. The apartment temperature dropped, but the fragrance lifted me. How it danced; how I danced with it—until I heard the neighbors.

"If you want to go to dinner, I'll get ready again," Lenni said, getting home from work. "You just have to say so."

From the bedroom, Kit said, "It's fine. I don't care. You never listen to me anyway."

"Just didn't know you made plans for us." A friendly lilt in her voice. Not flirtatious but caring.

"You know what," he snapped, "if it doesn't matter to you, I'll just go alone."

This was the decisive moment. That place in a conversation overheard that if you asked everyone involved to press pause, you could step into the middle of things. You could point at one opponent and then the other and say this: You have the option to move in one of two directions. One goes toward resolution, the other rivalry. If you choose resolution, all you have to do is say two words. *I'm sorry*. You can follow those two words with two more words, *I misunderstood*. Two plus two equals resolution. That simple. But if you choose the other direction, bypassing an apology, you are at risk of moving the conversation into very dangerous territory.

"What are you saying?" Lenni asked, stepping into their bedroom.

"I think I'm just going to go," he said, leaving the room.

"You don't have to ask me for permission. I'm not your

mother."

"You're not anyone's," he said.

"Don't even," she said.

"Now I know it was a blessing in disguise," he said.

"What does that mean?"

"You really think you would've been a good mother?"

"You arrogant asshole. He was saved from you," she said, as the front door closed.

Once, long ago, I assumed they lived a charmed life because of their beauty. His V-shaped physique, beard, and denim jeans. Lumbersexual perfection. But there was no one more stunning than her. As pleasing as a ripe plum. Soft and full and perfect at that moment.

How cruel life was to let us wait so long for love only to enjoy it with the wrong person. I wished it was still like it was, when I didn't know the worst of their relationship, when I only saw their clothes and exquisite furniture.

From their apartment, I'm sure they saw us as secondhand misfits. Mismatched kitchen chairs, an IKEA couch, a yellow Craigslist bookshelf, and the twin brass lamps bought new by a stranger three decades ago before we found them at a thrift store.

It wasn't that I was prying into their lives, but I was home all the time; and like a gardener, I watched them grow. Day by day. I was there when they moved in. How joyful. I was there when she miscarried. How awful. I was there when Kit was promoted and Lenni was fired and then re-hired, and I was there when their couch was delivered. A grand work of art that required four men to haul it into their building. The leather cushions measured four feet deep.

That day, I had run outside, tapping on the moving van's window.

"What kind of couch is that?"

"Restoration Hardware," said the driver, a man with a wide, porous nose.

"It's gorgeous."

His breath reeked of mints. "Gorgeous ain't cheap."

"No," I said. "Gorgeous is not."

He started the engine. "Now watch your feet before I crush you."

I searched online for their couch. From the Metropolitan collection. It cost the same as an economy-sized car. I imagined a hatchback parked in their living room.

But today, with Kit gone, she was all alone, like me. A special bond between us. Did she know?

If I could hear her, she could hear me. But I didn't say a word. Instead, I backed away and sat in bed. In the gray shadows, I listened to her cry. Not loud. But little interruptions full of breath. Inhaling deeply, and that rapid stuttering of a long exhale.

I reached to the nightstand without thinking. I was holding the meteorite, and in my hand the white veins throughout the black meteorite seemed to glow.

"It can't be."

The meteorite was warm again. I held it to my lips. Why was it warm? The lamp wasn't on and nothing on the nightstand was warm. But the heat came from within.

"What type of mystery are you?"

I searched for a reason online. Long-term exposure to low-level radioactivity disrupts electrons causing a reaction. This leads to glowing. And warming. Glowing rocks. Hot stones. Was this a chunk of some Chernobyl-like rock from outer space? What was I doing with it in the house? Next to our bed?

That was how my brain worked. Leaping from a headache to a brain cancer diagnosis. Howard would tell me I was being ridiculous. That a meteorite does not glow, and if it was glowing—

the glowing was an illusion. Light from somewhere else in the room reflecting against it. I was being ridiculous; I didn't need Howard to tell me. The rock had been in the sunlight. With the shades open, it had been warmed by the sun. The answer was simple.

My phone began vibrating. The suddenness startled me, and I dropped the meteorite—a sound of a far heavier object hitting the wooden floor.

"Hello?"

I heard breathing. Only breathing.

"Hello?"

The breathing ended. I could hear the blood pumping in my temples. And then a whisper, like a child's voice. But mechanical. What was it saying? The call disconnected, and I tossed the phone back onto the bed. It bounced lightly on the comforter, and a glint of sunlight flashed off the screen.

When I tried to pick up the meteorite, it seemed like it had doubled in weight.

"Are you okay?" a voice called into the room.

I looked at the phone.

But the voice was Lenni. I walked to the window. The crying had blurred her eyeliner.

"I heard something fall," she said. "Are you alright?"

"I'm okay," I said.

"You probably hear a lot you don't want to hear, huh?"

"It's okay," I said. "Mine hardly even talks to me."

"Trade?" Lenni asked.

"Sometimes silence is nice," I said.

"I'll have it soon enough."

She smiled. It was a genuine smile. Even on days like today, we can smile. Human connections. That was the best we could ask for.

Chapter 23

A parent visiting an adult child is an act of cruelty, really.

Those obnoxious roles of the past suddenly rear their ugly heads. The quick remembrances of the most embarrassing moments relived through every story. As if you stopped having experiences past the age of twenty. They continue to ask you: Are you still vegan? Because in high school you spent half the year protesting meat. They ask you: Why don't you find a nice girlfriend? Because for a time during your freshman year in college you dated women. They ask you: Do you still hide the peanut butter to keep from eating the entire jar?

But like it or not, they visited us in Portland.

It was the second time—the first shortly after the wedding. They had met boyfriends when I lived in New York, but I wouldn't characterize them as parents who were excited to have a gay son. Although they weren't downright rude to the men I dated, equally they weren't affectionate. But it was different with Howard.

The first time, Dad immediately joked with him, and Mom asked questions about his childhood in Wisconsin—if he preferred the snowy Midwestern winters or Portland's rain. Howard said both weather patterns were tied for last, but each brought out a desire to bake bread.

"Did I ever tell you," Howard asked her, "that my grandmother never bought a loaf of bread in her life? I remember her kneading dough every morning. In the dead of winter or when it was pouring rain, we wouldn't open the windows, and the entire house smelled delicious. You could taste the air."

"Isn't that a fabulous memory," Mom had said. "I'm going to remember that, if you don't mind. That will be a nice thing to think about later on."

I picked them up at the airport. Howard was home when

we returned. He shook Dad's hand, then hugged Mom.

"It's a nice building," Dad said, looking around. "Except it's in Portland. What about an elevator out front?"

"I could do without the stairs," Mom said. "Thom always wanted an elevator in our house. Like we were rich. He's always had an active imagination. What was your imaginary friend's name?"

"There's something different about you," Dad said.

Howard pointed to his face. The drooping eye lid, the sagging lip, and lifeless cheek. A face half-melted.

"Thommy said you weren't feeling well. You get that checked out?"

Howard shook his head.

"I don't blame you. I'm not a big fan of doctors. Thommy, on the other hand, he'd go to the doctor for a stubbed finger. Did you know he used to ride his bike to the emergency room every other week with these headaches? But they were nice about it. Gave him a Tylenol and sent him home."

"Come on," I said. "You don't think he should get it checked out?"

Dad waved off my suggestion.

"He's a grown man," Dad said. "He knows when it's time. Just last week, I slept wrong and the whole side of my face fell asleep. Like that all morning. Maybe you're sleeping on it wrong."

"Show him the gifts," Mom urged, and Dad opened his suitcase, presenting Howard with three jars of marinara sauce from different Italian restaurants: Bottisti's, Perreca's, and Cappiello's.

"I still remember how much you love bread," Mom said. "I thought, why not dipping sauce?"

"Don't let her fool you," Dad said. "She was hoping you'd open them for her."

"Oh hush," she said, smiling girlishly.

"And I thought you needed this," Dad said, handing Howard a sealed cardboard box. "Open it," he said.

Howard peeled away the clear tape. Inside the box was a firm blue plastic case.

"Every man needs one," Dad said. "Trust me."

After unsnapping the latches, Howard held up a power drill.

"Makita," Dad said. "Best on the market. Drill through anything."

"He was so excited to get that for you," Mom said. "And this too," she said, and from her bag she handed me a small velvet box.

"You used to love wearing it when you were little."

Inside was a thin gold ring. A perfect diamond mounted. I'd never owned a diamond. What did I need with a diamond? But I envied women in the TV commercials. A diamond is forever. The whole spiel and magic of the moment. So much emotion encased within one stone.

"But it's yours," I said.

"Don't tell your father," she said. "Do something fun with it."

I hugged her; she felt small in my arms. I'd heard about that point in a parent's life when they start giving away their things. Planning for the inevitable. They were both in their seventies. Not young, but healthy enough. Still a decade away from any serious complications. But the process had to start sometime, and it began with the gift of her diamond engagement ring.

"What's this about a meteor in Portland?" Dad asked. "It's all anyone's talking about back home. I told them I'd get to the bottom of it."

"It's nothing really," I said. "The size of a golf ball, but it broke a what's-it-called on the telephone pole."

"Transformer," Howard said, the word mashed in his

mouth. He pointed out the front window to the empty lot where the warehouse had been. Where the charred oak tree still stood.

"Right in your backyard, huh?" Dad said. "What do people think? Aliens?"

"Don't get him started. I'm hungry," Mom said. "It was such a long flight. They don't even give you peanuts anymore."

These were not the same people from my childhood. Their kookiness was a result of their diminishing mental capacity. All the spit and vinegar of their younger years was now a distant memory, because as they aged, visions of the end flashed in their minds. They imagined they could still alter their legacies—if they worked hard enough. But they were too old to leave any sizeable impact on the world, so instead they made peace with one another, then their only son, and finally his husband.

Before we could offer a tour of the apartment, Gordito ran into the center of the kitchen. He stood proudly like a tiny prize fighter—even without prompting him—his diamond-shaped tuft on display.

Mom screamed. Dad tried to kick him. But Gordito hissed and stood his ground.

Howard quickly scooped Gordito into his hands.

I said, "He's harmless."

Mom sat on the kitchen chair breathing heavily. Dad stood, poised.

I tried to explain.

"You don't need to explain," Dad said. "I get it."

"Our landlord tried to exterminate him," I said.

"You were always a sensitive boy," Mom said. "It makes sense."

"Too sensitive," Dad said.

Howard shut Gordito in our room.

"We should go to dinner," I said. "I think we all need some fresh air."

"I'm not leaving my things here with that," Mom said.

"It's fine," I said. "He's trained."

"Good … boy," Howard said.

"He's never destroyed anything of ours," I said.

"You don't think it's odd?" Dad continued. "Maybe I'm getting old, but maybe that thing has a disease. You ever think about that?"

I said, "There's a Thai place we've been meaning to try."

"We don't eat Indian food," Mom said.

"No chickpeas," Dad said.

"Okay," I said, ushering everyone out of the apartment.

Howard was quiet. He was thinking.

Dad said, "What about a steak house?"

"Or Italian would be nice," Mom said.

I rubbed Howard's neck as he locked the front door.

"They love you," I said.

"Easy," he said, "be… around."

"Well, that's certainly not true," I said, and soon enough, I was right.

On the sidewalk, the sun on our faces, a woman with a baby carriage passed.

"What a cute baby," Mom said. "It wasn't so long ago when you could look at a person and know if he was good or not. But now these terrorists, they look the same as everybody else."

"You mean white?" I asked.

"That's all I'll say about that," she said. "I don't understand the world anymore. Now what did I do with my purse?"

Howard pointed to her shoulder where it hung.

"Veal parm," Dad announced. "That dish seems to be going out of style. But I love veal. I won't apologize for that."

"My wallet," I said. "I forgot it inside."

Dad pulled Howard aside.

"This meteorite," Dad said. "I read a lot. Firsthand

accounts. Keep your eyes peeled, okay? That's all I'm asking. You two mean a lot to us."

Mom said, "He's not a child. It's Thommy you have to worry about. He's the one with the active imagination."

"Keep an eye on him. I mean it," Dad said to Howard, pointing at his good eye.

Hiking up the stairs, I knew my wallet was in my pocket. I inhaled deeply.

Even as an adult, I couldn't shed the anxiety. I wanted to confront them about everything, but in their presence, I was that scared, sensitive boy.

Breathing in, I feel peace. Breathing out, I know this is a wonderful moment.

And with that, I imagined a child reading a book on our couch. Our child. I would never be like them. I would be a good father. A great father.

With a sense of hope, I opened the apartment door.

"Gordy," I said.

Natural linen was strewn like confetti. Bits and pieces of Howard's chair and cushion stuffing everywhere. Holes were tunneled into the arms. Gordito poked his head from the birdhouse, his tiny black eyes unblinking. The pillows on the bed were torn, too, and the lamp on my nightstand was on the floor beside the decorative dish. Everything spilled. The buffalo nickel, the Turkish coins, the sunstone, and the meteorite.

There was too much destruction for the amount of time he was alone.

"What?"

Gordito stared at me the same way he looked at a peanut or the wall. I wanted some emotion, a sliver of remorse. Or understanding. But it didn't exist.

"Why?"

Then I did a strange thing. I reached for the meteorite first.

Of everything that was knocked over or broken, I was pulled to the meteorite. The white veins glowed. A band of light spread around the meteorite like a halo. The weight exceeded any rational expectation. It was the exact size as it had always been, but the weight had octupled. Impossible to lift with one hand. The surface was warm again, yet the window shades were drawn.

This rock, this thing was reacting. A defense. Like an organism feeding off our environment consuming energy to grow, not in size, but weight. The unknown physics of another planet.

With two hands, I pried it off the floor, and breathlessly set it on the nightstand. A tired creaking of joints beneath its weight.

The room was in disarray, but suddenly that didn't matter. I turned the conversation toward the meteorite.

"Did you do this?" I asked.

The white light intensified, and the meteorite pulsed. A sound like a beating heart. A dull *thump, thump* and a pause and another *thump*. Gordito watched us from his broken birdhouse. His head swayed back and forth as if he was able to understand the meteorite.

"Impossible," I said.

But the light grew more intense. Bright enough to force me to look away. I had no idea how to stop it. It wasn't Gordito who destroyed the room but the meteorite. I was sure of it. And now I knew what had to be done.

I opened the window. Ready to heave the meteorite back into the world for its second flight. But when I grabbed it, it was burning. Too hot to touch.

"You can't," I said.

I had no idea what I was dealing with.

Finding a metal spatula in the kitchen, I slid it beneath the meteorite, but it was too heavy. The handle bending under its weight.

"You can't. You can't. You can't."

Gordito didn't come any closer but watched as we fought. Watched, waited, and listened. He was a smart squirrel—wise to stay away.

But I had to pull it together. I had to walk away. *Clear your thoughts, Thom; deal with this later.* Right now, my parents were waiting. Howard was waiting. One thing at a time. Be present, be amiable, be well.

I will tell them Italian food sounded wonderful. I will tell them Gordito was fine. I will tell them everything was perfect.

And sometime tonight, I will have to tell Howard the truth.

But not right now.

50,000,000 ly

gravitational influence on us.

we can see a galactic interaction in the distortion

dissipate into the surrounding galaxy.

7,800 ly

750,000,000 ly

Chapter 24

Everything unraveled. First, Gordito was banished. It was Howard's choice. I couldn't tell him what I really thought, and I needed to know what role Gordito was playing. But without him, the world around us began to crumble. A week later, Kit and Lenni moved away. And over the next few weeks, Howard's condition continued to fail.

Amidst all this chaos, though, there was one triumph. The victory of knowledge.

I was a scientist, and this was my experiment. I hated being witness to this disintegration, but it was the only way to know for sure.

On the 21st day, I woke up with my final answer.

Howard wasn't in bed.

"Howie!" I yelled. "I know what's wrong."

I found him in the kitchen. The overhead light was off, and he was quiet, contemplative.

Howard sat at the kitchen table, and he wagged his index finger at me. "All ... under ... control."

"I mean it," I said, rubbing my unshaven chin. "I need to tell you."

"Me ... first," he said. "Doctor ... tomorrow."

"My god," I said.

He nodded once with authority, then turned his attention to his bagel, pinning it against the plate, as he finished buttering.

"That's incredible."

I thought about what to say. Or how to say it. I bit my lip. He tore the bagel as he buttered. It was supposed to go so smoothly. Knife. Butter. Wipe. But it tore, and the perfect bagel was no more.

"I found part of a meteorite," I finally said. "A while ago. And all this. I can fix it. I know how to fix it."

He stopped and turned. Knife in hand. In a scene from a film, he could murder me. Plunge the blade into my chest, and I would fall. Crying, wondering. Why? But this was not a film. This was me telling him a secret. *Please don't destroy me for my secret.*

"It's been causing everything."

The way he stared reminded me of the way Gordito looked at me from his birdhouse. Emotionless.

"I know what you're thinking," I said. "But I can get everything back to normal."

He closed his eyes and shook his head. I told him how the neighbors' fighting worsened after I brought it home. I told him how his condition declined after I brought it home. I even told him how Gordito's behavior went off the tracks after I brought it home.

"It's the only explanation," I said. "What else could it be?"

He placed both of his hands on my face. Like a father to a son. And he rested his forehead against mine.

"You ... Thom."

"Me?" I asked.

He nodded.

"How could it be me?"

"You," he slurred. "Force ... things." He rubbed his forehead back and forth. "Mind ... racing. Need to ... slow down."

"I'm not making this up," I said. "I saw it with my own eyes. It was glowing. I'll show you."

I grabbed his hand and showed him the meteorite.

"Touch it," I said. "Go on."

"Obsidian," he said.

"No, it's not. It's part of the meteorite. Gordito found it in the lot. He brought it to me."

As I was explaining, my words echoed through the room, or in my head, and I heard how it must've sounded.

"Take … break," he said. "Stress. Me … worry, Thom."

"Me? I'm the one worrying about you. You're falling apart, love. And I can save you. Don't you want me to save you?"

We stood beside one another in our bedroom, pointing at a stone and arguing about its origin. What had Kit and Lenni heard all these years? What had Kit and Lenni thought? Without context, we were crazy. I was crazy. But I wasn't crazy. Was I crazy?

Chapter 25

The neighborhood in the rearview mirror cut out the bad stuff. No gravel driveways littered with aluminum cans or plastic wrappers. No boarded windows or broken-down Pontiacs. A perfect, tiny glimpse of the world. Only a terracotta flowerpot in an empty Michelin tire, and red beebalm growing with wild abandon. Everything looked okay in the mirror.

But as we drove home from Howard's doctor appointment, I knew everything wasn't okay.

"Tell me exactly what the doctor said."

"Asked … hiking."

"Why about hiking?" I asked. "We haven't been hiking in how long?"

"Lyme … disease."

"You have Lyme disease?" I asked. "Is that what they said?"

Growing up in the Adirondacks, Casey—our dog—had ticks. We pulled them off with heated metal tweezers. But I'd not thought about Lyme disease in decades.

Howard shook his head. "Then look at face. Lift brow, show teeth. Frown."

"Why frown?"

"Rule … out," he said. "Bell's … Palsy."

"So, you have Bell's Palsy, too?" I asked.

Howard shook his head, again. He held out his hand to slow down, then pointed out the window. A coyote crossed a long grassy field. I'd heard about coyotes in the city. There was a news story a year ago about one stuck on the city train. The coyote was lean bodied and moved gracefully through the high grass. But it looked out of place. Clearly an intruder. What do wild animals carry with them from the forest to the city?

I stopped at the red light and gripped Howard's thigh.

"So, what is it?" I asked. "What do they think it is?"

Howard watched the coyote. Maybe his lip trembled. What was he thinking?

"Howie?"

"Come … back. More … tests," he mumbled.

"That's all?" I asked. "They couldn't tell you anything else?"

"No stroke … no Lyme … no Bell's."

"And now we just sit and wait? That's it? They expect us to sit and wait for how long? I can't believe this is our medical system. Should we see someone else?"

Howard placed his hand on top of mine.

"Not … young," he said. "Time … running out."

"It's not like you're going to die," I said.

"Me, you … talk family."

"That's what you want to talk about? We don't even know what's wrong with you."

The light turned green, but I didn't budge.

"Yes," he said. "But need you … better."

"Me better?" I almost laughed. "Me?"

"Yes."

"I'm fine, Howie. I'm great."

Cars began honking. A truck pulled onto the shoulder. The driver held up his middle finger. My foot still on the brake. It felt so natural to stay exactly where I was.

"Really," I repeated.

"Denial," Howard said. "Let … go."

Chapter 26

Let go.

I spent the morning driving around the city. Home Depot. The neighborhood tool shed. First Class Used Tires.

At home, I rolled the meteorite off the nightstand onto the nose of a hand truck. I chose a day Howard was out of the apartment—running his own errands. The neighborhood tool shed only had one hand truck with a U-Haul sticker. Tipping the nose up, the meteorite slid to the rear notch. It moved easily through the apartment, and at the stairs, I turned around and walked backwards, easing the truck down one step at a time.

On the sidewalk, white veins glowed in the sun. I dumped the meteorite onto the curb and piled a half-dozen Home Depot bricks and two terracotta flowerpots on top. I carried a used tire from the trunk of our car. It was beginning to look like an authentic mess. But I wasn't finished. I ripped the top off a bag of potting soil and poured everything onto the mound. Perfection. No one was going to confuse this with anything other than illegally dumped trash.

I called the Bureau of Environmental Services, navigating through their automated menu until I was speaking to a real person.

I said, "A pickup truck just drove onto the sidewalk and dumped junk. I can't tell what it is exactly, but there's broken pieces. Kids could get hurt. The pickup truck had a sticker on the tailgate. An ichthys."

"A what?" the operator asked.

"A fish," I said.

She asked me a series of questions about the amount of junk. The exact location.

By the end of the week, it had all been removed. The bricks, the pots, the tire, and most importantly, the meteorite.

Whatever it was doing to me and Howard, it would have to do from far, far away.

For so long, I longed for more excitement. Wishing for the end of monotony. For so long, I stared blankly at the computer screen, writing words for other people to read. Was that any way to live? I wanted to go back in time. Hit rewind and undo it all. Go back to before the meteorite and Gordito and the fire to when it was just me and Howard. Simpler times.

Of course, I knew I couldn't. Howard had been right; I wasn't fine. But I did what I needed to do; I got rid of the meteorite. I could now focus on living a humble future.

Chapter 27

It started with short daily walks, then longer walks. I stared at the vines scaling the building. Life living. They never stopped reaching, no matter how many times they were cut. The persistence of nature to continue; it would not give up. It had succeeded where I've been failing for years.

Behold, the inspiration to plant a garden.

I rented equipment from the neighborhood tool shed. A spade, a trowel, a red wheelbarrow, one hoe, pruning shears, and a dandelion digger. Researched the best ways to weed flowerbeds, edge sidewalks, and trim hedges.

It was a small yard, shared by the residents. I mowed in opposite directions, making a Y-shape at every turn, then mowed perpendicular to the original pattern and ended by mowing the perimeter once more and removing any irregularities for a perfect checkerboard finish. In the past, Armin—our landlord—hired a lawn service. But for a discount on rent, I offered to do it.

A woman—long, kinky white hair and whisper thin—watched from her first-floor apartment. She wasn't shy about her observations, standing at her window sipping from a mug.

As time passed, I thought less and less about the meteorite and more and more about the lawn. It needed constant attention; it needed me.

One day, the woman with the coiled white hair caught me on my knees holding a pair of pruning shears. I never engaged her face to face, but as I clipped the blackberry bushes, already overtaking the tomato vines, I knew it was her voice—the cadence and poetry in her pronunciation.

"A gorgeous day," she said. "I certainly never want to spend my time inside when all this is here. Give me the splendid silent sun, I say."

Shading my eyes with my hand, I smiled back.

"That's what I tell my Roger," she continued. "Forget the bad and remember the good. He'd be here with you if he was feeling better."

Then she told me her name was Sonia. Roger and Sonia had lived in their apartment since they retired two decades earlier. A second marriage for Sonia but a first for Roger.

"Is he okay?" I asked. "Roger?"

"I nearly mistook you for him. I thought my Roger took straight to his work without telling me. He always says he profits from his gardening days."

"I've definitely been profiting," I said. "I guess it's my therapy."

"Yes, well, it's good to see this yard won't go without help. An active mind is all one can ask for. Someone important said that, but I can't remember now."

"Amen," I said; it seemed like the right thing.

"I don't know what I'd do if my mind went," Sonia continued. "I'd just as soon walk in front of a speeding bus than live a day without it. I'm not even joking."

What a dark thing to say, I thought. *But what a beautiful white smile.*

Sonia was an odd woman; I liked her. She wasn't shy to speak her thoughts. There was no separate act of interpreting what she wasn't saying. Not like with Howard. Every conversation with him was a test of reading his mind.

"Let's hope it doesn't come to that," I said. "A speeding bus."

"Yes," Sonia said. "Of course, one can hope for the best. A very slow bus would be much worse."

This was how our friendship began. And now there seemed to be so much to look forward to. Daily I woke and spent an hour weeding with my morning coffee, and never a stranger, Sonia sipped her tea by my side.

Chapter 28

The neighbors' departure was unexpected. With so much happening in our lives, I had entirely missed what was going on. One day, two separate moving trucks parked outside. Loaded and left. Followed by an Alternative Meadow's FOR SALE sign.

Only their memories remained. For years I had listened to Kit and Lenni through their open window. Their growth and love. Their combat and quiet. Their fighting repeating like the seasons. Patterns of anger, peace, rebirth, and stress.

The first open house brought swarms of young couples. Producers, graphic designers, and software engineers—all sporting black-rimmed glasses and rainbow-striped socks.

After a few days, the condo was still for sale—a glitch in the system, because nothing lasted in this market. Everything overbid. Everything sold immediately. We even heard of buyers filming sad, pleading videos to persuade sellers.

As the days passed and the apartment was still for sale, I mentioned it to Howard.

"What about a fresh start?" I asked.

Howard had a blank gaze. I couldn't tell if I caught him off guard or if he was mad. Something about the new shape of his face.

"Why?" he asked.

"I know it's not far, but we like this area. And I've always loved their space. What do you think?"

His speech was coming back slowly, but he rubbed his chin and considered the idea. It wasn't like him to not have an opinion. And I wasn't that serious, but once I said the words aloud, they clung to me like a tick.

"It's probably expensive," Howard said.

"We could always see," I said. "Window shopping."

"You get obsessed," he said.

"I know," I said. "But I'm not obsessed with moving. Trust me."

I called the realtor anyway. She was delighted to hear about our interest.

"It's the perfect place for a couple or a young family," she said. "You're just going to live it. I mean, love it. Trust me!"

The day of our appointment, the sidewalk teemed with pedestrians. A crowd standing in a circle. A teenage boy raised his arms in the air, angling the lens of a camera into the center. The siren of a police cruiser grew as the car sped up the street. The crowd parted, revealing an old man lying prone, his arm curled like a broken wing under his chest. The cruiser stopped at the curb, and the driver rushed to the old man. Another car and a second officer hurried around the bumper, speaking in code into his walkie-talkie.

The boy with the camera had a pimpled chin and frizzy hair. He continued taking photos as one officer checked the man's vitals. He was awake, and he waved his free arm, swatting at the officer.

As a voyeur, I would have no problem watching a couple having sex at a club or dancing in the street or arguing in public, but it was too much to stare at someone incapable of standing on his own.

We weren't outside long, soon ducking into the apartment building next door. The realtor waited at the door. She held a compact to her face to double-check her makeup. She opened her mouth, her cheeks stretched back, making a terrible face. I watched for too long. Then she scratched lipstick from her teeth with her index finger and rubbed her tongue back and forth.

"Sorry, we're late," I said, interrupting her. "Someone nearly died outside."

"Good heavens," she said. "At least you two are okay, or I'd be waiting all day. Oh, it's a beautiful day, isn't it? Good enough to buy a new condo, I bet."

Howard smiled with his eyes. Charming Howard, was that who we were going to see today?

"Well, no one wants to wait around for nothing," she said. "Now, I might be mistaken but you two are brothers, am I wrong?"

She was petite, in a white jacket, matching pants, but to push against all the sameness, she wore paisley pumps.

Why would she say that, I wondered. We looked nothing alike. Especially now.

"Married," I said.

"Married," the realtor said, clapping her hands together. "I just knew it. That was my second guess."

Gold balloons spelling HOME were taped to the wall in the kitchen.

Howard tugged the **0** balloon as we passed, and it suddenly lost air, letting out a strange noise, and the balloon slowly, slowly shrank.

There was a pause, before the realtor said, "Strikingly similar features, though. I've heard people tend to gravitate toward those who look like themselves. But where are my manners? You can call me Marsha. That okay? Now let Marsha show you around. This beautiful two-bedroom has tremendous lightning, just tremendous. Did I say lightning? I meant lighting."

"It's nice," I said, looking at Howard to gauge his interest. "Right?"

"You know, the previous owner worked for Nike, and he said the *lighting* was perfect for computer work. What a funny thing to say."

Howard palmed his cheek.

Or irritated Howard, I thought. *Maybe we'd see that version today.*

Leading us through the kitchen, Marsha said, "Now look at

this," fanning her hand across the space. "This is the only time I ever get to feel like Vanna White."

"Why did they move?" I asked.

"Oh heavens," Marsha said. "This condo is owned by a very impressive man, but he lives in the Bay. The tenants, I think, now I could be wrong, he was offered a job in Paris, France. She was a model, his wife. Fashion, that sort of thing. Imagine being a model in France? Très chic."

"Teacher," Howard said. "She was a teacher."

It seemed like overnight he learned to speak again. The garbled, mashed words of last week, or last month, all straightened themselves out. The only change was the meteorite—some unknown force infecting him that was gone. And he had me to thank.

"We live next door, but we weren't close," I told Marsha. "I think she was a college professor, is what he means."

Marsha said, "Oh, that's right. A schoolteacher. I meet so many people selling real estate, it's hard to keep everything straight. Harder than you'd think."

The kitchen and master bedroom were much larger than ours, and the second bedroom was bright with natural light.

"The owner has impeccable taste," Marsha said. "He's from Geneva. If you were thinking of buying, now's the time. The time has never been better, I can assure you."

"You said the Bay before," I said.

Howard huffed loudly.

"Did I?" Marsha asked.

"My … gosh," Howard said, and put his face in his hands.

Why was he acting like that?

"Howard," I said. "Stop it."

The way he looked at me. And Marsha too. Why were they both looking at me like that? Like I'd done something wrong. Like I was the one who guffawed and gestured in annoyance.

"What?" I said.

But they kept looking at me.

"What?" I repeated.

It felt like the world was going to spin off its axis. The ceiling, the walls, the floor. A spinning dreidel. Colors and textures blending until everything was gray and frothy. And I was standing in the center of a giant, empty valley of dead volcanoes, impact craters, and lava flows. It could've been the surface of the moon. I looked down—at myself. My body was black and shaped like a stone. In my mind I was the meteorite.

"What am I doing here?" I called out.

The words were hollow and echoed back, but when they came to me, they weren't the same words.

Escaping is not the answer.

They were crystal clear.

"What?" I said.

Change will not solve your problems.

"Then what's the cure?"

Happiness is not a checklist.

With a place to call our home, a partner by my side, I've always found a way to feel alone. As quickly as the fantasy appeared, so too was it snatched away, and reality came rushing back. On Earth, they were not staring at me. Howard and Marsha. In fact, they had both wandered off, and I was alone in the spare room.

I caught up to them in the master bedroom, where I found a calendar tacked inside the closet. The date, May seventh, circled and colored in pink highlighter. It was already June—the date long passed. Kit and Lenni didn't strike me as a "colored in pink" couple, but the wide looping curves of each letter was feminine. Lenni had written the word *freedom*.

"When did they move out?" I asked Marsha.

"In May. The start of May."

"May seventh?"

"That sounds about right. But like I said, it's so hard to keep up with everything when I'm making so many sales."

"She planned it," I said to myself. "That's what she was talking about. She was counting the days. That's what she meant when she said she'd have her silence."

Marsha's phone chimed "Uptown Girl," and she excused herself, stepping into the hallway.

Howard rubbed his eyes, then looked at me. Softly. He held my chin in his hand and frowned.

"Can you really see us here?" he asked.

"Can't you?"

He turned his head away.

"I know this won't solve our problems," I said.

Gazing out the bedroom window that connected our worlds, our apartment appeared small, unkempt. Gordito's sliding door on our window was locked, secured with duct tape.

Looking into our bedroom, we had only made half of our bed, the sheets spilling out from beneath the comforter. My dresser drawers were not entirely flush. A stack of unread books towered on the floor, but the tidiness of Howard's side created a different reality. He was the neat one. The one with a plan. He had wanted to get married. He had wanted the child. A paint-by-numbers approach to our relationship. Up until now I had just gone along with it, but was it what I wanted? He was such a good partner in so many ways, at least from one angle.

On his nightstand was a framed picture of his nephews, a tube of lip balm, a historical novel with a bronze bookmark. This is how Kit and Lenni saw us. I was the mess. But I didn't believe it. I wasn't such a disaster, and he wasn't so perfect. I could see there was a richness to the mess. A series of parts to be identified, arranged, and pondered. On my nightstand, three books on Portland's history, two about Chinese immigration, and one on California's tech boom, which brought fleets of newcomers to our city. It was all interconnected. There was an order to everything if you looked hard enough, close enough.

But from here, no one was the wiser. If this wasn't us, then who was it? I had created an entire narrative about Kit and Lenni based on their clothes and furniture. Based on snippets of their worst conversations. Based on a word she had written on a calendar. *Freedom.*

Was I wrong?

Staring into our apartment, I knew we had a life together worth living if we could decipher the code. A language of desire.

Our mess could easily be sorted—it had all the potential in the world. But in our neighbors' apartment, we would have to start from scratch. And I'm not sure Howard or I had that much energy. The world we created together in our tiny apartment was nearly finished.

Howard hugged me from behind as I stared into our room.

I rested my head against the good side of his face.

"All I ever wanted was to sleep well. Maybe a vacation every year. Simple stuff. Maybe write a book someday. I can't think of anything more that would make me happy. Maybe, you know, like you said—we could be fathers."

I clutched his hand. The realtor returned to us.

"You two look perfect in this space. The light in this room would make an amazing portrait. It's really tremendous lightning, isn't it? There I go. I said it again. Lighting, I meant. I hate to say I told you so, but when it's true, it's true," Marsha said.

"It'll be perfect for somebody," I said.

And Howard agreed.

We left, and the crowd on the sidewalk had cleared. It was a sunny day, and I watched two squirrels chase one another around the charred oak tree. Neither of them was Gordito. They spiraled the trunk in one direction and then the other. They were

fast and svelte, playful in their fighting—at the very beginning—
still waiting to fall in love.

Book II

Chapter 1

The kettle whistled. Bitter tea bags floated in our mugs—vessels older than our relationship.

My mug was born in Upstate New York from the hands of a potter who sold his wares at the Saratoga farmer's market. An unassuming mug. Brown glaze exterior, but it was the inside that caught my attention. Galactic swirls of variegated blue formed a small universe. Steam no longer rose from the inside of that mug, but I held the world in my palms as I sipped lukewarm tea.

Howard had found his mug at Goodwill. *World's Best Urologist.*

He tore a hunk from his cinnamon raisin bagel, and I reached for the other half.

"I haven't been myself in months," I said. "But seeing our apartment through the window like that. It made me realize we need to start living. Don't you think?"

Howard leaned back in his chair.

I said, "This isn't about moving either. We need to shake things up. Can you do that? Can you be spontaneous with me?"

He crossed his arms. Maybe he didn't get it, or maybe he didn't care.

"You know what I mean," I said.

Howard yawned. Was he intentionally being difficult?

"Maybe I'm not making sense," I said. "But I want to make things like they were. I don't mean go back. But feeling you beside me. Being a unit, like we used to be. Don't you get that?"

"I get it," he said.

"Sometimes I don't think you do," I said, and I found myself shaking. "I feel like I'm going to break apart."

"Come here," he said.

It had been a long time since I sat on his lap. I pressed into him like I was pushing through him. I didn't speak. Nothing. As if the sound would mean everything would end.

We tried to make love. It wasn't what it used to be. Howard had lost the ability. Only a memory now in a photo album where the pictures had been. Instead, I tried to focus on gratitude. What we have, not what we want. Not what I want. Rediscovering an old appreciation. Our bodies touching, our breath connected. Pure energy not driven by lust but an acceptance that we wear and tear. We break down. But we weren't broken down.

In bed, with my head on Howard's chest, his armpits smelled piney and sharp.

"I think I'm really ready now," I mumbled.

Howard combed his hand through my hair and rested his palm on my neck, a gentle massage.

"For a kid," I continued. "We lost so much this year, and I need to add something back. We do, don't we? We can't go on losing things."

He tugged my hair, craning my neck, and stared at me.

"You mean it?" he asked.

"I do," I said. "I really do."

He reached between my legs. Skillful fingers rubbing, tugging, and petting. He pulled me into him. Is this what it felt like? You say the word child, and something is released into the world. Something born. It wasn't about sex but the potential to have a child. Our child. Grinning foolishly, I held my breath. And when I couldn't hold it anymore, I came inside him.

"Boom," I said. "You're pregnant."

Of course, he wasn't pregnant. That wasn't how it worked. But I wondered—in a different world where that was possible, where I could impregnate him—what would that feel like to create a life—in this exact moment?

"I wish," Howard said. "But when do we start?"

"Tomorrow?" I asked. "Today."

Chapter 2

When I was twenty-two, I read *On the Road* and *Into the Wild*. Cross country road trips and hitchhiking defined a life worth living. I had worked as a barista, and to earn extra money I bought blowout sale books at Barnes & Noble and resold them on eBay for twice the price. All to buy a ticket to Anchorage. My thumb led me to Seward, Homer, Talkeetna, Fairbanks, Juneau, and Valdez.

In those days, I dreamed of being a writer, because being a writer meant having an uninhabited escapade, and it meant drinking too much without judgement. Living through the vice was the expectation. And if anyone was up for that challenge, I was.

When the wheels hit the tarmac at Ted Stevens International, the flight attendant told us the local time and the temperature in both Fahrenheit and Celsius, as if nothing else was more important.

My first stop was to buy a bottle of Jack Daniels. But I was confused; the price tags in Alaska were double. Or more.

"Why?" I asked the cashier, a woman my mother's age.

"State taxes hard booze to high heavens to control the depression. And the suicide. And domestic violence, too. People still buy it. But you know what they say about a poor wife-beater?"

I didn't know, but I nodded.

"Here's your change, sweetie," she said. "Enjoy your night. No beating up on your wife either."

For two months I was Alexander Supertramp; I was Jack Kerouac. Sleeping in hostels, or in my tent on a spit surrounded by white capped mountains. I drank bottle after bottle of expensive Jack Daniels, but all I wrote were a few drunk poems on the backs of napkins and a handful of postcards to my parents.

When I returned to the Lower Forty-Eight, I stopped hitchhiking, but I continued drinking. Drank through a graduate degree and all the way back home to New York. I felt at home at every bar in Saratoga Springs. Teaching college courses by day and drinking into the night all while telling tales of my brief life on the road. I wasn't Alex Supertramp or Jack Kerouac; I was Henry Chinaski.

Every night ended with barflies complaining about having no money, but I'd tell the story of the bald eagles entangled in a death-drop under a midnight sun. I never saw it happen, but a long-haul trucker who gave me a ride from Fairbanks to Little Gold witnessed it, and he said they were fastened to one another—a few seconds of sweet love before releasing mere feet from the ground. Or else I told one about a grizzly bear standing roadside, waving at the traffic that passed him—all loners of the back country. Or else I told anyone who would listen about my whiskey sticker shock. Astronomically priced Jack Daniels sold by a woman who could've been my mother. The sticker shock story guaranteed one more round before the night ended.

That was the last time I had true sticker shock.

Until now.

Child adoption fees.

Howard and I assumed a couple thousand dollars. Never expected twenty or thirty-grand. We spent hours online. Hundreds of webpages offered advice. The more we learned; the less we knew.

No idea if we wanted a newborn or a toddler. Domestic adoption or international. We didn't know if we were willing to adopt another race. What gender do we pick or was there gender variance? Did we prefer to go through an agency or an attorney?

Howard poured two glasses of Cabernet. I didn't drink like I used to. Too many blackouts; too many forgotten nights; too many mornings waking up alone in bed with spent condoms like shotgun shells on the floor.

"Can we get a loan to buy a kid?" I asked, my legs stretched across two couch cushions with my laptop on my belly.

Howard tapped my legs, and I swung my feet to the floor.

"I found a questionnaire." I showed Howard the website. "Like a *Cosmo* quiz but for the perfect child. Stuff like what foods they eat, how athletic they'll be, preferred sexual orientation."

Howard scratched his head.

"Doesn't it feel like a sci-fi movie?" I asked. "Today, we're picking our perfect baby. But what if we don't think it's perfect a year from now?"

Howard said, "Maybe there's a warranty."

I drank my wine and then his. I thought we were having fun, but we'd never had this conversation. Words baffled us, eluded us.

"I'm not Catholic, but I think I want him baptized," I said.

"He?" Howard asked.

"Or she," I said. "I can't explain it. I'm just telling you how I feel."

We scanned website after website of adoption agencies. The data blurred—a sea of potential children for us to choose from for the right price. How much was a child's life worth?

Chapter 3

Sonia and I talked about books, her childhood, how she met Roger, and how he was still sick but feeling a little better. We talked about what it was like to live through so many decades of every kind of injustice and inequality. I told her about Howard, his problems. I didn't tell her about Gordito. Some things had to wait.

"There's something about getting outside," Sonia said. "It helps me relax. I think it would do wonders for everyone. There's a name for it, I just can't remember right now."

I pulled weeds, and we talked about extraordinary things and the mundane, as if everything was equally important.

"Did you watch the Leonids?" I asked.

"I can't remember," she said.

"The meteor shower," I clarified.

"Fascinating," she said, but she had no recollection.

"That's around the time Howard started falling apart."

"Interesting," she said.

She wasn't ignoring the fact that Howard was falling apart, but she helped see it as a natural state of things.

"That's why we moved to Portland. To be free of judgement," Sonia said. "You know how it is around people who don't accept you. That's how I felt in Port Townsend. But Roger and I could start over here. You can't control people, but you can control yourself."

I said, "I just wish I could help him. But I hear what you're saying, I can't control everything."

"Forest bathing," Sonia blurted. "I learned about it when we were in Japan. Roger just loved their soup. I found their politeness refreshing. But yes, the only thing you can control is you. And the rest, well, you have to accept it."

"Even if he never gets better?" I asked. "We've been to the

doctor. But they can't pinpoint what's wrong."

"That keeps me up too," Sonia said. "But with Roger, I ask myself, what does better mean? Does it mean what it was like in the past? Well, if I'm honest, that disturbs me. Quite literally shakes me to the core. Because nothing good came from the past. So, I put my faith in the future."

"What will be, will be," I said.

"Que sera, sera," Sonia said.

I bent over, inspecting the rhododendron. I'd bought pesticide when I noticed mysterious mites—red-bodied with white pin-legs—that had been eating the foliage. Dozens moving from one leaf to the next. Leaving them ravaged and holey.

"Spray a light mist around any flowers," I read aloud, from the back of the pesticide bottle. "Avoid the base of the bush and the roots."

"All these natural things," Sonia said, as if ignoring the crude act that I was engaged in. "They live and move in peace. Isn't that remarkable?"

I wiped a bead of sweat from my eyebrow. "I get the sense that if I spray this on anything else, I'll kill half the yard."

"My heart leaps when I see how it all fits together. But Roger always said the world is too much with us in it. That's just it, isn't it? That's life."

"It says it's just moderately toxic if eaten, absorbed, or inhaled."

"Thom, can I ask you a favor? A small favor, really, if you could spare a moment."

I took off my work gloves and sat cross-legged in the grass. "I guess the mites can wait," I said, delaying their execution. "How can I be of service?"

Her apartment was small but filled with a lifetime of stuff. Every inch of the walls hung a picture frame. Cabinets stacked with knickknacks: porcelain dogs or owls, holiday cards, half-burned candles, even tin tobacco canisters with the words "Hindoo," "Troutline" and "Flick and Flock." Each tin had a distinct hand-painted quality: two dogs in profile or a man fishing in a creek.

Sonia pointed at the tins. "He just adored the pictures."

"Is he home?"

"Didn't I tell you?" she said. "He went in for some tests. They want to keep him overnight."

She opened a closet door, pointing at the top shelf. "It's the green book. With the velvet. Do you see it?"

I raised my arms and stood on tippy toes, sliding the photo album from beneath a box.

I said, "Next time ask for something hard."

"Let me show you something. Do you have the time?"

She opened the photo album, turning page after page. Each one filled with memories faded from the passing years.

"This is what I was looking for." She tapped a picture of a young woman—hair dark as midnight—riding a farm tractor. "That's how I learned to drive. My father told me the standard transmission in our tractor was identical to a car, so every day he let me help him in the fields. I know he wished for a son, but all he got were girls, and the work needed to get done. I learned to drive, which back then was a big deal. Especially for girls like me. Not like today. Girls today, well, maybe everything turns out exactly like it's supposed to."

"I bet it seems like a different world today," I said.

"You'll never guess what year this was." Sonia peeled back the plastic sleeve to show me the date on the cardstock, but as she did, the adhesive on the plastic wouldn't release the emulsion—tearing the image: half of her face and chest in the plastic, half on the original paper.

"Deary," she said, laying the piece flat to make herself whole. "Would you look at that?" She lifted the plastic, again. "A woman of two minds."

Her laugh was genuine.

I said, "Maybe we can scan it. Have it digitally corrected."

She scrunched her nose. "I've never heard of such a thing."

"These old albums," I said, "they're incredible, but we could digitize the entire thing."

Sonia closed the photo album.

"Everything is changing so fast. You wouldn't believe it, but you'll see. Someday someone will tell you that everything you thought you knew was wrong. Digitize the book, then what kind of artifact is that?"

"I already feel like everything is all wrong," I said.

She said, "But that's just it, isn't it? That's life, too."

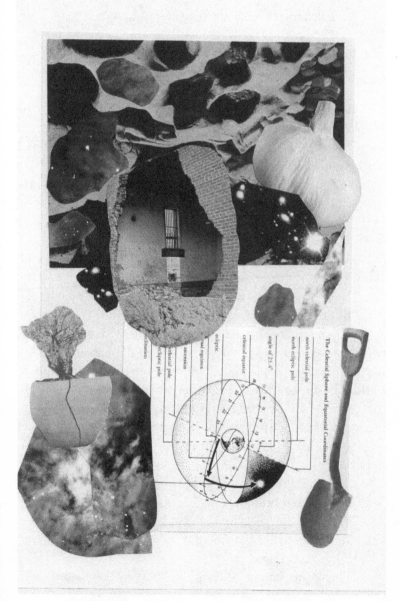

The Celestial Sphere and Equatorial Coordinates

north celestial pole

north ecliptic pole

angle of 23.4°

celestial equator

ecliptic

vernal equinox

ascension

celestial pole

ecliptic pole

clination

Chapter 4

A week later, I received a note at our door.

The best thing about life is living it, and yet all the suffering gets done by the ones who keep breathing.

Roger had suffered a heart attack, and while he was in the hospital, he'd endured a second episode.

Howard was opening cupboards searching each shelf as I read her note. He set a can of *Spaghetti O's* on the counter. He only ate Spaghetti O's when he was upset. We had no savings. He had no idea how we could afford adoption fees.

"You're not going to eat that. It's a thousand percent of your daily sodium."

"Maybe if we put a hundred dollars aside a week," he said. "Or we could sell your mother's engagement ring."

"Not now," I said. "Roger, her husband. He's dead."

"But the diamond ring," he said. "It's perfect."

He was right. The diamond engagement ring was exactly what we needed to sell to make this next phase of our life become a reality. While we had moved from the "pit stop" phase to the "flat-lining" phase, we were now past all of that. Our life together had a pulse again, and we were edging into the "family" phase. It would be impossible without money. The diamond engagement ring was part of the answer, but it was not the time to talk about it.

"Can we talk about this later?"

"Later," he repeated.

"Promise," I said.

We walked to her apartment. When Sonia opened her door, I said, "I'm so sorry."

"Thank you, honey," she said, holding my hand lightly. "It's not like I haven't thought of this day a million times. That's what it's like getting old."

"Whatever you need," I said. "We can help."

She seemed exactly like she always seemed. Perfectly accepting of the situation.

"I'm not sure we've ever met," Sonia said to Howard. Her kind eyes traveling over his face. "My Roger was a handsome man in his younger days, too."

If Howard could've smiled, he would've. Instead, he took her hand and brought it to his lips.

"Oh, you," she said.

Howard glanced into her apartment. Curious now. She told us what happened. She told us that she could accept that some events are uncontrollable. But what bothered her the most was that she was alone. Not without people but without someone who understood her.

"It's a selfish thought, I know," Sonia said.

"It's not," I said. "Like your note. The suffering happens to those of us who keep living."

"Maybe I shouldn't ask," she said. "You didn't know my Roger, but I have a feeling he'd fall head over heels for the both of you. He had a lot of very close male friends. Would you like to attend his service?"

She explained that her son lived in Seattle but traveled for work as a Business Manager for a software company. Roger was his stepfather. On their last phone call, Sonia's son said he needed to finish a project in New York and couldn't rush home. She confided that it hurt, not because he wasn't there for Roger, but because he wasn't there for her.

"It'd be an honor," I said.

Howard squeezed my hand.

"But won't the rest of your family wonder who we are?"

"I didn't think of it like that," she said. "Neither of us has a very large family. That's still alive, I mean. And my son, I told you about him. It's complicated."

"We'll be there," I said.

"Everything comes back," Sonia said. "Everything. I truly believe that."

Built in 1923, the Guild of St. Sebastian Sanctuary had an arcaded entrance, curvilinear gables, and radiated a history of pomp and grandeur. I felt like a stranger—in body and in spirit—staring at the stained-glass window. Christ knocked on a door with no handle. He wore a crown of thorns and a ruby-red robe. In his other hand, he held a lantern, shining and bright.

Listening to the eulogy, Howard fidgeted, massaging his hips.

I was happy that Sonia asked us to be here with her. Until this year, we were strangers, but I imagined if anything happened to Howard, I wouldn't know who to ask for help. Maybe it was easier to let a stranger into your life during a crisis—they hold no history or judgment.

The priest spoke of nature. He sermonized, "Grass is a symbol of life and death. Yet the smallest sprouts show us there is no death. That life does not wait to begin again. Growing onward and upward. And to die, it does not mean to end. Like the great humanist poet Walt Whitman wrote, 'To die is different from what any one supposed, and luckier.'"

Howard patted my knee.

When the priest spoke of Whitman, I couldn't help but see him differently. He was a handsome priest. Age had changed his appearance—the elasticity of his cheeks and neck loosening— but his face held hints of his past self. His clear eyes. His devilish smile.

Howard pushed on my leg again.

"What?" I asked.

"I need to move."

I angled my legs, and he excused himself. "Now? You can't wait?"

He shook his head. "Hurts sitting."

I didn't say goodbye to Sonia but followed Howard, listening to the priest's voice trailing behind me.

"The rest is up to us," the priest continued, "the living. Balancing this grief with our hope. It is love that creates balance. Love that is fully accepting of the darkness and the light within each of us. The living and the ending. Yesterday and tomorrow. Love is the thread that connects all people through all points in time."

I thought of my own funeral. *Who would leave early?*

As I followed Howard, I imagined the ghost of Roger sitting in the rafters, watching us. I said to myself, *I wanted to stay, Rog, but you get it, life is for the living.* The ghost of Roger would understand. He sat peacefully, grinning. Maybe sympathetically. Like I was the one he should feel bad for. Like I was someone who should be saved.

Before I fully exited the narthex, the priest's last words were, "Don't focus on the door that's closing, but the one that will open. While we don't know half of the world's mysteries and we wander in the dark, we shall continue onward, seeking the light."

Chapter 5

Life was for the living.

Neither of us had the right boots or moisture-wicking shirts. No Smartwool socks or cargo shorts. No daypacks or trekking poles. But that didn't keep us from hiking Angel's Rest. The trailhead was full of Outbacks, Renegades, and shuttle buses. All of Portland was here, but we parked in the second to last spot. Every year we talked about hiking, but time passed, and all we did was talk.

A group of teenagers started the two-and-a-half-mile hike the same time as us. Their slim bodies sweet-smelling of cheap perfume. Beneath it, an undercoat of sexually charged sweat.

"Is it a tough hike?" I asked one of the boys.

Tall and muscular, the boy resembled the statue of Apollo. He said, "I dunno, *boots*."

"Do we need boots?" I asked.

"Damn, *sis*," the boy said, shaking his head. "*Boots*, not boots."

"I think *boots* means something," I told Howard. "What could *boots* mean but boots?"

Howard raised his palms.

"Does it bring you back?" I asked. "They've got their whole lives ahead of them."

"Some already know what they want," he said.

"I still don't know what I want."

"It's apparent," Howard said. There was a lightness to his voice. Was he teasing me?

Through a canopy of broadleaf maple and fir trees, the trail moved through a series of boulders before rising to a bluff. We were within earshot of the teenagers ahead of us and two men speaking Russian behind us. The simple smell of the trees and ferns and the unevenness of the ground underfoot reminded me that our world was not all bike lanes, wine bars, and deadlines. This other wild world governed by its own rules. Amongst the quiet leaves and the gentle breeze, I still knew that every day nature fought to survive. The teens laughed incessantly, screamed involuntarily. The two men speaking Russian laughed, too, but they never screamed. And in the hidden depths a white-tailed deer slept and a mountain lion hunted.

"It's weird this mountain is in the same world as the Burnside Bridge. The opposites, I mean. I forget the rest of the world exists sometimes. Don't you miss touching things? Like really feeling them?" I wondered aloud. "I swear I never touch more than my keyboard and my phone."

"Can we slow down?" Howard asked.

I set my palm on a tree trunk, bark like alligator skin. Howard stopped; he drank from his water bottle. I carried on a few more steps, and Howard waggled as he walked towards me.

"Are your hips okay?"

He grimaced. "Maybe it's going to rain."

"We can go back," I said.

"Go on," he said. "I'm fine."

The view overlooked Beacon Rock, a massive plug from a volcano, and Silver Star Mountain's exposed, bald peak across the river in Washington State.

"Maybe," I said, but I stopped myself. He knew what was right for him, and if he needed to go to the doctor's again, he'd go to the doctor. Maybe my father was right. Or maybe I just couldn't argue about it right now.

The men speaking Russian passed us, followed by a trio of women my mother's age.

Howard waved his hand at me, as if to say, "I mean it, I'm okay." But the pain on his face as he walked, the tightening of his jaw, told a different story.

I said, "We shouldn't have come here. But god, I wanted to

get outside. Why is it always so difficult?"

We were like two squirrels chasing one another around the trunk of a tree, and the tree was Howard's failing body.

Then I said, "Just for the record, I don't think this is your fault."

We didn't speak again until the peak.

Ralph Waldo Emerson wrote a poem called "The Mountain and the Squirrel," where a mountain and a squirrel recognize the limitations of one another. The squirrel couldn't carry a forest on its back, and the mountain couldn't crack a nut.

I couldn't help but think of our relationship—all its limitations. All the reasons to break up rather than endure. Maybe that was what a longtime relationship was—regularly talking yourself out of running away.

"You like the view?" I asked. "It's unexpected."

We stood an arm's length apart.

"Maybe not the view," Howard said. "But how we got here."

"That's what you like?" I asked.

"No," he said. "But it is unexpected."

We were no longer talking about the hike. Howard sat on a boulder, taking in the scene. The teenage boy—the young Apollo—tapped Howard on the shoulder. He held out his device.

"Mister, will you take our picture?"

Howard looked at me, then back to the boy.

The boy said, "You cool, *boots*."

They all huddled together. The boys held up their middle fingers and stuck out their tongues while the girls puckered their lips. They were children, but they wanted to show the world that rules didn't apply to them.

I wanted to believe that our lack of intimacy was not his fault but nature's. His urologist had told him that erectile dysfunction was common for men his age. Stress related, most likely, but there were pills.

Descending Angel's Rest, thoughts about other men crept into my mind. Harder men. Bigger men. Any men. I reminded myself that our relationship was more than sex. Life, at this point, was more than sex. Maybe that was why it was easier to imagine a child. To replace what was gone.

Chapter 6

It had been two weeks since we promised to help Sonia. Howard carried the tray of lasagna—a recipe from my mother. But when I called her for it, she had said it was from *Joy of Cooking*. That was what Sonia needed—something comforting. It didn't matter where it was from.

I said to Howard, "Remember to be nice."

"You don't have to tell me," Howard said.

"She means a lot to me," I said.

The table was ready for a feast. Plates and candles. Three different forks and spoons. If I could measure the distance between items, I had no doubt it would be perfect.

"It smells heavenly," Sonia said, peeling back the tin foil.

"His mother's recipe," Howard said, winking at me. "She's quite a cook."

"Really from a cookbook," I said. "But it reminds me of home."

"Oh, there's a word for that," Sonia said. "But this mind of mine."

She plated our food, and I looked across the silverware, selecting my middle fork, as Howard chose the longest. Sonia opened a bottle of red wine and poured three full glasses. She placed a metal stopper into the bottle.

"What are we missing?" she asked, returning to the table.

"It's perfect," I said.

Stevie Wonder played on the radio. The bassline and piano. That voice. Singing about New York City. Sonia's head swayed. I liked watching her caught in the moment.

"This song," she said, lifting her wine glass. "When I was a little girl, we used to listen to this song. My parents hardly spoke English, but they could hum along. There was a station in Aleppo that played this kind of music. It sounded like another planet. All those buildings and people. You can imagine my surprise when we moved to a farm in Washington. It was the strangest place I could've ever dreamed."

"You're Syrian?" I said. "I never thought to ask."

"You can't ask such questions," Sonia said. Her teeth were beginning to stain from the red wine. "But that was a long time ago. Now I'm just me."

When Howard set down his fork for the last time, Sonia said, "Well now, I guess the night's not getting younger."

I said, "You got us as long as you need us."

We followed her into the bedroom. In contrast to the impeccable table setting, the bedroom was an entirely different scene. Cardboard boxes piled in the closet. Paperwork and folders spilling from the dresser onto the floor. A heap of men's leather shoes in the center of the rug. It smelled like mushrooms. Her room had been ravaged without purpose. This was the other side of perfection.

But what was most odd were the three tree branches beneath the windowsill, like a make-shift teepee. Were these the signs of mental deterioration?

Sonia carefully laid a blanket over the branches.

"One of Roger's projects I can't get rid of. But the rest, well, I just don't know where to start. Maybe you have an idea? I don't know if it makes more sense to start with the biggest or the smallest."

"Maybe the shoes," I said, because they were the closest. "Do you have a garbage bag?"

"Maybe you could look through them in case you want to keep any. Roger certainly doesn't need them. But if you don't, I understand. Maybe you want Roger's rocking chair? It's an antique. There's a mark somewhere. You'll see the maker's name."

A gorgeous chair with a floral motif carved throughout—

deep within the headrest and armrest. I couldn't say if I'd ever looked upon a more beautiful chair.

Even Howard agreed. "It's a ravishing chair."

"I can't keep it, but I don't know how to get rid of it," she said. "Does that make sense?"

"We couldn't accept it," I said.

Then, with a smile, Sonia said, "Okay. Fine. It goes to the dump."

It took us two and a half hours to box and bag all of Roger's belongings. There was power in sorting one's possessions. The painted tin boxes. The clothes and shoes. The decorative ashtrays and carved wooden pipes. We were determining what would stay and what would go.

"I don't mean to pry," I said. "But I smell mushrooms."

"Roger's jerky," Sonia said. "He makes mushroom jerky. I'm sure you could take some."

"I don't know," I said. "Maybe we're okay."

We loaded the car and returned for the rocking chair and then again to say goodbye. The front door was wide open.

"Did you leave it open?" Howard asked.

"Hello," I called.

"Back here," Sonia said. "Roger's home."

I turned to Howard, who shrugged.

"What does that mean?" I asked.

Sonia sat in bed, staring at the corner of her bedroom and those three branches. And there he was.

Gordito.

Standing on his hind legs, he reached for a strip of shriveled mushroom jerky hanging from a limb. There were a dozen shriveled mushrooms. But that was not what caused me the greatest alarm. In the center of the teepee—a shimmering black stone.

"It was the strangest thing," Sonia said. "The day Roger died

144

this little angel showed up. I knew it was him because Roger loved collecting rocks. He showed up holding the most beautiful stone. See it?"

Gordito crawled toward the meteorite.

Why was it here? And then I heard it. *Thump, thump.* The undeniable voice of the stone.

"Do you hear that?" I asked.

"Hear what?" Howard said.

"He finds the mushrooms outside," Sonia continued, "and hangs them here. You know when I was a little girl, we hung meat in our garage, and every Friday my father got his paycheck and he'd buy potatoes and cut some meat into cubes and we'd have meat gravy. I don't know what Roger is doing with these mushrooms, but it just feels right. Go ahead and pet him," she said. "Roger doesn't mind one bit."

Howard's eyes smiled from corner to corner. He was genuinely happy to see Gordito, and he bent down onto his knees and reached for him, but I shouted, "Be careful!"

Howard leaned forward.

It never occurred to me that Gordito had assumed another residence.

I didn't want him to touch the meteorite. I didn't want anyone to touch the meteorite. Just as Gordito had brought the black stone to me, he now offered the stone to Sonia. There was a pattern.

"Oh, and watch this," Sonia said. "Roger, are you ready?"

Sonia shuffled beside Gordito. The two of them faced us.

"I taught him our routine," Sonia said, and Gordito nodded, just like I had trained him to.

Together, in perfect unison, they took one step forward. Then one step to the left. Then one step back. They raised their hands above their heads and wiggled their hips. Sonia grinned, and Gordito's mouth curled upwards. They came to a full stop and clapped once. Then continued their routine in the opposite direction.

Whatever move she made, he made. Whatever move he made, she made. They were one and the same.

Howard applauded. He wiped a tear from his cheek. I'd not witnessed this happiness in a long time.

"Bravo," he called. "Bravo!"

Sonia bowed, and Gordito bowed.

But I couldn't take my eyes off the meteorite. Glowing. Faintly. I was sure of it.

"If I'm … honest, I had … hesitations about you," Howard blurted. "But … this. Well … speechless."

"We need to go," I said.

Sonia said, "But we have another one too."

"Please," Howard said, nodding.

"No! I said no!"

Gordito blinked rapidly. For a moment I thought he would pose, like a boxer, but he scratched his head. Then he eased back down and crawled behind the meteorite. White veins glowing brighter.

"Howard, please," I said. "Can't you see what it's doing?"

"Why … hurry?"

"Can't you hear yourself? It's happening again. We need to go," I said, and I left them standing in her room. "Howard," I yelled back.

Chapter 7

Planning a future implied being alive to live it. We weren't vegetarian, or avid joggers, or yogis; we didn't schedule regular doctor appointments or wear sunscreen or drink eight glasses of water a day; we didn't count calories or workout; we were "normal Americans," which meant we were not all that healthy.

Howard pushed the grocery cart, and I scanned the aisles. We conferred over every item at Trader Joe's.

"Last night," I said.

"Was wonderful," Howard said.

"No," I said.

His sentences were back.

"You're too competitive," he said. "What she was able to teach him in such a short time."

"I'm talking about the stone. I got rid of it."

"The obsidian?"

A woman in yoga pants, a tie-dye tee, and a sun hat stared at the shelf of red marbled steaks in plastic wrapping.

She mumbled, "If I eat a hundred and fifty calories in the morning, skipped lunch, I can have a burger and water, but if I want a hard kombucha, then. . ."

"It's not obsidian," I said, reaching for a packet of seitan. Red meat would now only be for special occasions.

"What's obscene?" she asked.

"Sorry, I was talking to my husband," I said.

"I can't decide," she continued. "Is that paleo? I only eat paleo, except Wednesdays when I don't. Then I'm gluten free."

I scratched my cheek, and said, "There's a diet for everyone."

"Really?" A lilt in her voice. "Do I look like I diet?"

I wasn't sure if I was supposed to apologize, explain myself, or walk away.

"So judgmental," she said. "I can't stand it."

Howard interrupted, wiggling a sleeve of cinnamon raisin bagels.

"Are you one of those gluten-free haters?" she asked. "This is harassment."

I said to Howard, "Let's go."

"It's this city," she said, talking to the shelf of red meat. "The moral fabric has dissolved, and this is what we're left with. No one can save us."

Standing in line to check out, neither of us talked about what had happened. Maybe I thought she'd hear us, sneak up behind us, and launch into another argument. Everything seemed like an argument. With her, with Howard. He needed to understand how serious the matter was—the situation at Sonia's. How could I explain it so he'd actually hear me?

Crossing the parking lot, a silver Audi blared its horn.

I froze, but Howard turned. I expected to see her. Following us. Filled with rage. But the driver, a man our age, waved at us to get out of his way.

"Maybe that lady was right," I said. "The moral fabric has dissolved."

As we drove home, I told Howard a story from my childhood.

"It's weird, I never thought about men. Not until I got tangled up with this older guy who worked at the roller-skating rink. It wasn't even sexual at first. But he flirted, and no one had ever talked to me like that. That's when everything changed. Like this place, at some point someone flips a switch, and the lights either blast on or everything goes black. Either way, it's absolutely one hundred percent different. That's what last night was. The light turned on, Howie."

"What do you mean?" he asked. "You're talking in circles again."

"That wasn't Sonia," I said. "I know Sonia. And that was a different person. But I don't think it's her fault."

"She lost her husband," Howard said. "It can be a lot to process. Let her be who she needs to be while she grieves."

"I don't think you understand," I said. "I've been dealing with this type of thing all my life because I've never really understood who I was. But when I knew I knew, and before that, I just wore masks. Last night was a mask."

"What's this have to do with Sonia?"

"Not Sonia," I said. "The meteorite. It's got some sort of hold on us. You have to believe me. It's dangerous."

Chapter 8

National Suicide Prevention Week.

Hourly, the public radio station played commercials for the suicide hotline. I never knew anyone who committed suicide, but a high school classmate of Howard's jumped off a bridge in the middle of winter. Somewhere in Wisconsin. The story goes, he jumped feet first through a gap in the ice. I imagined he met the water with nearly a splash and sunk faster than his breath whooshing from his chest. I wondered what he saw while plunging. Water transforming from emerald to a numb shade of navy. Specks of light flashing across his vision like blinking fireflies in a field at midnight as the oxygen in his blood thinned.

Howard and I listened, and we gardened. We planted neat rows of garlic, and Gordito watched carefully from the edge of the lawn as we raked loamy soil with our fingers, dropping cloves, then repacking dirt and slapping the earth with every success.

"Can we talk?" I asked.

Howard placed a clove, the pointy end up. He didn't pack the hole but motioned for Gordito, who tiptoed closer, lifting the garlic into his mouth, his cheek bulging.

"I think it's connected. Gordito, Roger's heart attack, us."

Howard frowned.

"You have to let me finish," I said. "I'm thinking clearly. I swear. I won't even bring up the meteorite."

"You mean the obsidian," Howard said, even though his heavy lower lip was getting in the way again. After all this time, we were both used to his changing face.

"Since you brought it up," I said. "Yes."

Gordito shifted the protruding clove in his mouth as Howard stood up, wiping the dirt from his knees.

"I'm not making this up," I pleaded, kneeling beneath him. "You saw it at Sonia's. But I got rid of it. I put it out on the sidewalk and called the city to take it away. And they did. But now it's back. How is that even possible?"

Howard raised an eyebrow.

"You sound crazy," he said.

I said, "I never told you, but it's what made Gordito destroy our room. I should've told you, I know, but I know how it sounds, and I knew what you'd think, but I can't stay quiet, Howie. I'm serious. The meteorite is evil."

"You should eat something," he said. "We've been out here for hours."

"I'm not hungry," I said. "I'm angry."

"Then I'm hungry," he said.

I know I sounded crazy. But it was all in front of him, too. Why didn't he see the reality?

We spent the rest of the day navigating around one another like orbiting planets. Dinner, watching TV. There was only one way to deal with this hiccup between us. I opened a bottle of wine. After two glasses, I tried to break the silence.

"Truce?"

I offered Howard some wine, but he pushed my hand away.

"I don't know if we can survive another year," I said.

We had good days, even great days. But this was also us—an endless negotiation of miscommunication.

When the temperature outside dropped, Gordito visited our window. Staring into our bedroom. But he was not allowed—not with the meteorite so close.

My only victory was to shut him out, fearful that he'd carry the alien stone back into our home. But as the weather turned worse, Howard—without asking—unsealed the sliding door.

Reuniting with Gordito again brought Howard immense happiness. So much that it seemed to improve his condition. More talkative and smiley. I weighed the greater evil. The

Craig Buchner

potential of Gordito bringing the meteorite home or shutting him out and severing the few loose threads that kept us together.

The birdhouse had long been donated to Goodwill, but Howard would not leave him homeless. He cut a hole in a shoebox, like he had done in the beginning, and spread a hand towel across the base, angling two small sticks to hang mushrooms.

Gordito found fast comfort in his box.

I bent to one knee, peering inside, but it was too dark. I shined a flashlight into the hole, and like a spotlight, the white orb captured Gordito crouched in the corner, staring back at me. There was no black stone; I had to be sure.

Howard took the flashlight from my hand and wagged his finger at me.

"He's sleeping."

"No, he isn't," I said.

But Howard pointed at the box, motioning for me to look again.

Peering inside, Gordito had clustered his towel like a nest. Eyes closed, kicking his feet. Running in place. Chest beating, heart thumping. Chasing a dream in a dream. What did he see?

"How did you know?" I asked him.

It was as if we were moving on a vinyl record. Us and this city and time and space. And the needle was picked up and dropped along a different groove, because Howard looked at me strangely. One eye closed. Was he squinting or had the meteorite taken control of us? Lifting us from one space and setting us down in a different room where Gordito slept peacefully.

I said, "It's here. It has to be. Tell me, Howie, or it's going to get worse."

Gordito woke and peered from his box. Black eyes on me. Howard too. Both scanning me.

"There's nothing here," Howard said.

"We need to get help," I said.

"What kind of help?"

"Or we'll end up like Sonia. Her mind is going."

They both shook their heads no. They were connected. First, Sonia and Gordito and the dance performance. And now Howard and Gordito. What Howard did, Gordito did. And vice versa. Moving their heads back and forth and back and forth. The room became so small. Like the inside of a shoebox. Their judgement cornering me. Back and forth and back and forth and back and I pushed my fingertips into my eyelids, waiting for the phosphenes, but I still saw them, back and forth and back and forth and back and forth, moving me through time, and pushing even harder the phosphenes never appeared—only them—back and forth and back and forth and back and forth and back and forth, and I knew it was the meteorite, back and forth and back and forth and back and forth and back and forth and back and forth and back and forth and back and forth and back and forth and back and forth, and I needed to wait it out, and back and forth and back and forth and back and forth and back and forth and back and forth and back and forth and back and forth and back and forth and back and forth, and I wouldn't let it win, and back and forth, and it had to set us back down where we were, in our room where everything was normal, and back and forth and back and forth, and what was normal anymore, and back and forth and back and forth, and I don't know if I could tell which world was the right world to end up back in, and back and forth and back, and I needed it to stop, and forth and back and forth, and right now, and back and forth, and now, right now, and back and forth, and now and now and now, and why wasn't it stopping, and back and forth and there he was again—Howard.

"Are you okay?" he asked.

"I'm fine," I said, lowering my hands, blinking. "A headache is all."

"Maybe enough wine tonight," he said.

"You're probably right."

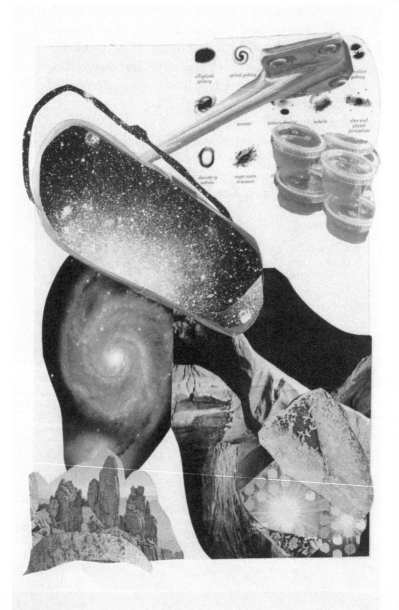

elliptical
galaxy

spiral galaxy

peculiar
galaxy

quasar

galaxy cluster

nebula

star and
planet
formation

planetary
nebula

supernova
remnant

Chapter 9

The garden thrived: squash, eureka cucumbers, and bell peppers. Between the buildings, bright green tomato vines tangled thorny blackberry bushes.

I had to get away. Outside. Away from the power of the meteorite.

Gordito roamed the yard, nibbling without worry, but I ignored him.

Something about nature blocked the meteorite's power.

The vegetables invited birds, but instead of scavenging, they brought their riotous chatter. The "wik-wik wik" of a northern flicker overtop of the "coo-ooo, coo, coo, coo" of the mourning dove or the "yeeps" of our American robin contending with the spotted towhee's "meow."

But I couldn't stay outside forever.

After an hour of gardening, I showered. Thankful to be home alone. To have space. Not expecting a knock at the door. Towel around my waist, I stepped on the cold tiles praying it wasn't the Mormon boys. Instead, a man at the front door extended his hand.

Half-nude, I clutched the towel to my skin.

"Sorry," the man said, shielding his eyes. He stood a half-foot taller than me. His dark hair cut at perfect angles. Metropolitan. Very expensive. But his eyes were bloodshot. A symptom of exhaustion or intoxication. He didn't wait for me to speak but said, "You probably know why I'm here."

"Are you okay?" I asked, concerned for his eyes.

"I'm Razi. You know my mother."

"I'm sorry. Who?"

"Sonia's son. Razi."

He said his name with the distinction of a Caesar or a Napoleon.

"Razi," I repeated. "Sonia's son."

After hearing her name, I saw part of her face. The nose—upturned. The flawless skin. Not a blemish or wrinkle.

"It's a sensitive matter," he said. "You have something that belongs to my father."

The way he spoke reminded me of a boss I had. A short man who I'm sure suffered from all sorts of personal conflicts. But Razi was imposing.

"Let me get dressed. I'll just be a second."

Razi wore a jacket and tie. He yanked up his sleeve and looked at this watch. A silver Rolex. "I don't have time."

"But my towel."

He exhaled. "If I'm on the highway in twenty, I'll be in Seattle by…" He counted to himself. "I have exactly five minutes."

"I'll be quick," I said.

He sat at the table. From the bedroom, I listened to him, the steady tambourine of his palm against the kitchen table. An aleatoric beat. A rhythm John Cage would be proud of, but I got the sense Razi wasn't the artistic type.

"You want a beer?" I called. "Or wine? I think we have an open bottle in the fridge."

I knew he wouldn't yell across the apartment.

"Or tea?" I said, returning.

"You know my mother," he interrupted. "So, you know about the squirrel. Sonia didn't say much, but it's a shame what you did. Begging her for the chair."

"I'm sorry, what?"

"She's a sick woman and having a pet like that. They carry disease. She said it was yours."

I said, "To be frank, it seems like you're accusing me of something."

He said, "Then you steal my father's chair. I should call the police."

He stopped himself, closing his eyes. His lips began to move, counting to himself before he said, "I took her back to Seattle, and now I'm taking my father's rocker."

"Sonia's gone?" I asked.

"Don't tell me you sold it."

"What do you mean you took her?"

Razi said, "Now she can get the attention she deserves. She's sick, but I'm sure you knew."

"She never said a word."

"Her place was a mess. You'd be crazy if you missed the signs."

"Honestly, I had no idea." I sat at the table with him. But then I remembered having that exact thought. Seeing the tree branches in the corner of her room. At first, I had thought it was mental deterioration, but then I saw the meteorite. "She told us it was going to the dump."

He stood up and said, "I don't want to make this more difficult than it needs to be. But I can call my lawyer."

"Take the chair," I said. "We didn't want it. She insisted."

"Uh huh," he said, looking around the apartment.

"Can I at least call her? I need to know what she did with the meteorite."

"The what?" he asked.

"Did you find a stone? A black stone," I said. "Under a pile of sticks."

I realized how it sounded. Asking him if there was a meteorite. Telling him about a pile of sticks.

"I'm beginning to get angry," he said, counting to himself again.

Howard didn't believe me; now Razi didn't believe me.

We stood a few feet apart, but in the greater scheme of things we stood worlds apart. "If I can just get the rocker, I'll be on my way."

"It's in our room."

"Perfect," he said, but I cut him off at the bedroom door. "Let me clean up."

He said, "Really. I'm in a hurry."

"It's private," I said. "Please."

I closed the door and hid Gordito's shoebox under the bed. The rocker meant nothing to us, but to Razi it did. How sick was she? I carried the rocker back to him.

I asked, "What do you mean sick?"

"Dementia," he said.

"Dementia?"

I watched Razi carry the rocker to the sidewalk. It banged against his SUV. I knocked on the driver's side window.

"What?"

"My number. Can I give it to you?" I asked. "If you find the black stone. I'm serious. I think it's radioactive."

It was the only way to convince him. But he raised the window without a word.

As he drove away, I held up my middle finger.

Dear Sonia, I thought, *sweet woman, poor mother.*

Behind me, sitting on the sidewalk, was Roger. At least, I imagined it was Roger. If he was really there, he'd open his mouth, but nothing would come out. He'd turned toward the sky, staring at the great wildness of that wild outer space.

"Tell me where it is," I'd say.

And Roger would extend his arm, pointing back at our apartment. Posing too long, like a statue from another time.

160

Chapter 10

The letter in the mail—it was completely unexpected.

Armin the landlord's writing. His unique letter ℸ with the two perpendicular lines, like a telephone pole.

I offered the letter to Howard, but when he reached for it, I never let go.

Dear Thom and Howard, This letter is to inform you...

I waved the letter in the air. "You think it's the ferret's dad? We should poison him. God, I wish I had it in me."

Howard turned away. No matter who he was or what possessed him, he was all I had. And right now, we were still on the same side.

This letter is to inform you that the residential property 1735 SE Morrison St. has been sold to Neourban Renaissance, LLC. All tenants will be required to vacate the leased-out premises December 31 for major construction efforts to revitalize the structure.

On their website, Neourban Renaissance claimed to usher traditional buildings into the modern age.

"What if we made an offer?" I asked Howard. "Is that a thing people do?"

Howard rubbed my back, as if to say, *slow down; you're doing it again.*

"People buy things all the time. This is a sign. And I know what you're thinking, that's not how signs work," I said. "But signs are whatever you want them to be."

In my mind, the plan was entirely possible. We'd buy the building, renovate each apartment, transform the commercial space. Maybe lease space to a doctor, again. I saw the tattoo studio as the perfect free clinic. The furniture store would be a bookshop. And we'd rent the upstairs apartments to low-income families. It would be perfect.

But if we did nothing, Neourban Renaissance won. We would be thrown out, and they would jack the rent.

"Fuck it," I said. "Maybe Portland's not for us anymore."

My mind was racing. I didn't think we were better than anyone else who would come to live in our space, but I weighed the impact. What we gained and lost as our city grew. The displacement of artists, day laborers, freelancers, single parents, the elderly, and adjunct professors. Portland politics supported these changes. Meaning the wealthy. It was becoming a tech town, which meant online innovations boomed. Not only for us, but everyone. This made for easier banking, investing, car services, food delivery, dating, marketing, photography; but how did all that technology nourish our soul? Emotions withered on the vine. We were addicted to the screen, scrolling through texts and tapping random images, because if I scrolled through a feed, I could fend off thinking about this shitty fucking world.

"What about Astoria? It's on the water. You need a drink? I need a night out."

It was too much to handle. There was no end to the obstacles. I had an urge to open the window. I needed fresh air. I couldn't breathe.

"Get your jacket," I said.

On First Thursday, art galleries across the city offered free drinks and hors d'oeuvres. The Elizabeth Leach Gallery bustled with art majors wearing black-rimmed glasses.

A group surrounded one artist who only went by Betsy. Boots and black coveralls. She looked like a soldier, and she lectured them on her piece—an American flag glued to a gessoed canvas. I vaguely remembered Jasper Johns' *Flag* at the Philadelphia

Museum, but Betsy called her piece *Think Again*.

"Seeing a painting of a flag begs the question if a painting is a painting or if a painting is a flag. But today seeing a flag on the back of a red pick-up doesn't symbolize freedom. It begs you to think again. Some of you want that flag destroyed. Some of you want that person destroyed. So, the flag changes. Flags on pick-up trucks or on bikinis or a napkin that you throw away. How many of you have ever done this?"

After the gallery, we met Azalia and Sky, my larimar witch, at Crush. Over pints of Guinness, I told them about Gordito. It seemed like the most interesting thing in my life without analyzing all of Howard's ailments in front of them. They didn't seem to notice or care. But the room was dim. And I couldn't talk about the meteorite. Not out loud.

We ordered another round, and I told them about the housing dilemma—the eviction, and after our third round, I brought up Sonia and Roger and Sonia's son, Razi.

"He had the gall to drive here from Seattle to ask for his stupid rocking chair," I said. "We didn't even want it. I should call him. Give him a piece of my mind. How can I find his number?"

"Life is certainly twisty-turvy," Sky said. "But they have websites, you know? It's like five bucks and you can pull cell phone numbers, criminal histories."

"My girlfriend swears by that," Azalia said. "For online dating."

Sky said, "Think about all that's happened since we met. You should call him."

"I know," I said, holding her hand, but she pulled away.

"What's his name again?" Sky asked, looking at her phone. "I'm going to find him. You can't trust anybody these days."

Then Azalia said, "Talk about criminal, just last week, did Sky tell you? They've been miscalculating our paychecks. An accounting error. They said it was a computer glitch."

"Oh brother," Howard said.

Sky was wearing her larimar and rubbed the stone between her fingers. "They blamed it on computers," she said.

I think Sky would believe me, I thought.

"I just said that," Azalia said. "Whatever software they use pushed a few dollars into every paycheck, nothing noticeable, but it's been five or six years. And here's the kicker," Azalia continued. "They're making us pay it back. Like we had a choice in the matter. How much do you owe, Sky? Three grand?"

Sky said, "But we can use our vacation time to pay it off, if we want."

"There's only one cure for this," Howard said. "Jell-O shots."

I shook my head. Maybe if I just blurted it out. Maybe that was how you introduced the unbelievable into a conversation.

Sky smiled at me and said, "I need a blue one. It's calming. I think you do, too."

"I like your eyes," Azalia said to Sky, turning her face from me, and they kissed.

I leaned into Howard.

"It's nice," I said. I don't know if I believed it or not. "This feels almost normal."

"You're drunk," he said.

"Maybe," I said. "But it's still nice."

Two rounds later, I pushed my credit card across the table. "Put it on me."

I felt a hand on my neck, and I heard that familiar laughter. Antonio. He looked drunk and happy. I explained that he used to bartend at Crush, but now he owned a food cart and sold fried chicken the way his grandmother taught him in North Carolina.

Antonio said, "I was the one who poured their drinks the night they met. You think it's arrows that Cupid shoots, honey? Oh, no. It's whiskey."

Sky asked Antonio which part of North Carolina he grew

up, and Antonio told a story about Durham fried chicken and kissing cousins and a closeted Methodist minister. Everyone laughed.

Howard left for the bathroom, and I asked Antonio if he wanted to join us for a cocktail at home.

"You think that's a good idea?"

"Howie won't care."

"Believe you me, angel eyes, I hate to say no, but whatever's going on with you two, I don't think I'm the answer."

"You don't know what you're talking about," I said. "We're fine."

"I know what I see."

"Malarkey," I said. "One hundred percent science fiction."

Howard touched my shoulder as he sat down. I tilted my neck into his meaty palm. He smelled like soap, and I kissed his skin.

I said, "You didn't miss anything, darling."

"Not a thing, pussy cat," Antonio said. "Like the French say, Dors bien."

"We should go, too," I said.

Sky hugged me—pressing hard into me.

"You need to take care of yourself," she said. "Whatever's happening with you, it's not good."

"I'll be okay," I said.

"If you need to talk," she said.

"I know, I know."

Sky said, "I just sent you Razi's number. Now you can go home happy."

We got home after midnight. Immediately, Howard opened Gordito's window, but he was nowhere. Howard set a few peanuts on the ledge and called Gordito's name.

"He must be on vacation," I told Howard. The words spilled out when I drank. "Where do you think he'd go? Someplace warm, I bet. Maybe Mexico or Cuba. Wearing a Tommy Bahama shirt. I can see his cheeks bulging with coconuts, can't you?"

We stripped down to our underwear.

"What if something's really wrong?" I asked Howard, lying beside him. "You know, doctors don't know everything."

"They know enough," he said. "They'd have called if it was serious."

I could smell his armpits. Strong, like curry. The collective smell of us, and the booze on our breath. Mildly repulsive. We didn't need to impress each other. Sometimes we could be ourselves, and that was good enough.

"We're falling apart," I told him. "Do I seem broken to you?"

He touched my forehead and said, "Not physically."

I nodded. "But if I'm broken inside and you're broken outside, what do we do? Can we bring a kid into our home like that?"

"I can't talk about it now," Howard said. "Not when you're drunk."

Holding my hand to my chest, my heart said, *"Thump, thump."*

"I never thought it'd be easy," I said. "But I never thought it would be this hard."

"Shhh," he said. "Go to bed."

Sleep folded over us. Heavy and woolen. And we stayed like that, unmoved all night long until the first signs of light filtered through the blinds.

To avoid waking Howard, I carried last night's clothes into the kitchen and dressed by the front door. I was positive he would still be asleep when I returned with pastries and lattes.

For a week it had rained, but today the sky was faultless. The air was cold but dry and blue. There were birdsongs—a collective chorus for some miracle. That was when I noticed it.

In the road, the carcass of a squirrel. My first thought was Gordito. The squirrel was chest down. Clearly dead for hours, maybe a day. I had watched the landlord scoop their carcasses up so many times with his shovel, but all I had was a gardening hoe from the community toolshed. The squirrel was the same color as Gordito, which made this act all the more devastating. Yet it had to be done. *A friend of Gordito's was a friend of mine*, I thought, and gently slid the end of the gardening hoe between the tiny, beautiful creature and the asphalt. Lightly I pried him from the road. As he peeled away, he flopped to one side, and I had the strangest feeling. It was not déjà vu but seeing the diamond shape on this squirrel's chest was too convincing. A doppelgänger. *Of all the squirrels I would find*, I thought, *I come across another with a diamond chest, exactly like Gordito's.*

Then it dawned on me. The truth was this was him. Even when I knew it was true, I struggled and told myself it wasn't. I lifted him in my hands. He was stiff, and his weight was unlike when he was alive—not an ounce of energy circulating his muscles. Time slowed. My thoughts. God. This. Why? How? Please. Breathe. This is not real. This is *too* real. His silent body. The ringing in my ears.

Howard breathed quietly in his sleep as I laid Gordito comfortably in the shoebox, covering him with his towel. Half-whisper, half-sob I spoke his name.

Chapter 11

In the shower, velvet steam surrounded me in a cocoon. I couldn't face him right away. Tell him the awful news. I twisted the handle even further to the left. The hot water stinging my skin. I remembered something from long before Gordito entered our lives. The first time Howard told me about his hips. I'd nearly forgotten. We had just woken on a Saturday morning. Before coffee, before brushing our teeth.

Howard stretched his legs long. Rubbing them hard, and then in frustration, hit his arms on the bed.

"Maybe you're arthritic," I said. "It's the rain."

He said, "It's hereditary."

"If you're worried, go to the doctor," I said. "Maybe they're connected. The hips... the fact that we don't... as much as we used to."

That didn't go unnoticed—not to me. Our life was simple enough that a pattern should emerge, if I paid close enough attention. If the pattern began with his hips and the pain meant we lost sleep then losing sleep meant touching throughout the night was lost. And when touching was lost, fucking was lost. And when fucking was lost, our patience with one another was lost. And when patience was lost, easy communication was lost. And when communication was lost, productive talk about starting a family was lost. And when talk of a family was lost, we were strangers living under the same roof. All because of his hips.

But in the steamy bathroom, the fan diffusing the mist, I stood with goose-bumped skin. The intense heat of the water on my skin made me aware of the cold air when I opened the curtain. That abundance of heat created its opposite. Systems connected to systems. Everything controlled by some other power. But what balance was restored by our strangeness to one another?

If that was how life worked, one thing and its opposite holding each other in equilibrium, then for every loss there was a gain, for every pain there was a joy.

The morning Howard told me about his hips, we eventually got out of bed and listened to NPR—a story about a musician. I drank coffee out of Howard's favorite mug—*World's Best Urologist*—but we didn't talk about going to the doctor for his hips. Instead, we listened to the news story about a musician named Phil, whose wife had died of pancreatic cancer.

"I couldn't imagine," I said.

"At least it wasn't so sudden they couldn't spend time together," Howard said.

"Is that supposed to be a silver lining?"

"I'm saying I'm glad they had time to say goodbye."

The musician named Phil carried on and used her instruments to record a collection of songs about her death all while raising their one-and-a-half-year-old daughter. As our great poets say, "life and death go hand in hand."

Something happened in the musician named Phil's past that rippled throughout his life. Unknown and unseen for years. So tiny. So unspectacular. Like pain in the hips. It eventually grew and emerged, and he found himself writing the saddest music he'd ever know.

"It's a bad world, hard to love," he sang in a clip.

That was how these patterns worked. They begin somewhere. And Gordito was now the start of what was coming.

Where did it begin for us? The chaos. Was it the meteorite or Howard's hips or earlier?

I knew that our life was complicated. I could never predict how we'd move from one place to another because any slight change would make for an incalculable shift. What was that inconsistent variable? Or who?

I didn't know it then, what would become of us. The

nowness. How whatever we were doing that day while listening to the musician named Phil would lead to this moment in the shower, about to tell Howard that Gordito was dead.

If you subtract something from this life, what was gained? How would those things negate one another to create order?

That day, thinking about the musician named Phil and his wife's terminal cancer, I turned the radio off before any tears formed in my eyes. Maybe I was the balance on that day, the extreme opposite, saving my sadness for later. Because now, I turned off the fan—naked and goose-bumped—standing on the bathroom mat and those tears reemerged.

Chapter 12

The intolerable shine of the cockcrowing sun and the excessively sweet smell of flowers in the air. I yearned for garbage and rot and hurt; the day did not deserve lilacs. Hardly able to walk a straight line, I couldn't make the call in the room with Howard. Seeing his face when I said the words, again: "He's dead." Not without cracking in half.

Under that careless sun, on the sidewalk, I watched cars pass. Straight-faced strangers driving through their own lives. Their own thoughts bouncing through their heads. Not one of them had my thoughts—not this moment.

Gordito was so much more than a squirrel; he was a future.

Razi answered the phone, and I said, bluntly, "He was hit by a car."

It was the only way I could get all the words out. To just spill them fast and sort out any expectations later.

"What? Who is this?"

"Sonia's neighbor. From Portland. Is she there?"

There was a pause. For a moment, I thought the call had been disconnected, but then I heard him breathing. It was a few seconds before he spoke again.

"Why would you say that?"

I said, "I want her to know he was hit by a car."

"How do you know?" he asked. "How did you find out?"

I said, "Because I found him."

"Him?" Razi asked. "I'm talking about my mother."

He wasn't understanding me. I should've been clear from the start.

I began again. "Your mother had a pet squirrel. I'm calling to tell her I found him last night. He'd been hit by a car, and I know how it ended last time, between us, but I had to tell her."

There was a longer pause. A muffled noise.

"My mother's dead," he said.

"Huh?"

That wasn't possible. Sonia could not be dead. I just saw her. How long ago was it? A couple months maybe. Was it longer? She had moved to Seattle. Yes. She was in Seattle, and she was being cared for. She was not dead. I was calling her in Seattle.

When the call disconnected, the meaning and the words finally connected.

"Dead?" I asked the empty air.

In almost all tragedies, it was better to hear of the news secondhand. Not in the room beside that person, to see their skin, to smell their breath, to hear them say, "It's happening." And watch the end of their energy. But I wished I could've been with Sonia. Her grace was extraordinary, and I knew she could've taught me something about passing to the other side.

I walked alone for some time. The neighborhood continued to be the neighborhood. The trees continued to be the trees. Almost every house had someone inside who went about their day. Unphased by what had happened to Gordito or Sonia.

But what really happened to Sonia all the way up in Seattle—one hundred and eighty miles away?

Our apartment was dark. Quiet. With the lights off, the shadows were a lead blanket and beneath them hid the monsters of the world. Because in the dark lurks the things we don't talk about. Any one of them could destroy us, so we keep them a secret, buried. And we walk around them until we've convinced ourselves they don't exist.

But not today.

I would find it.

It could not stay hidden forever.

I opened the cupboard doors, pushing the boxes of pasta and bags of half-empty rice aside. Knocking the cans of halved tomatoes and garbanzo beans onto the counter. I opened the refrigerator and yanked the meat drawer open and the crisper too. The egg container only had three brown eggs. There was nothing in the oven.

Where was it?

Howard was still in bed. Either asleep or listening. I was making too much noise for it to be considered regular morning noise. What did he know?

When I opened the bedroom door, he sat up. A penumbra of light across his body.

"Where is it?"

He shook his head.

"Does that mean you know and you're not telling me?"

I pushed over the hamper, then opened the dresser drawers. Throwing underwear and socks across the floor. Howard didn't move. Instead, he sat there and watched as I piled t-shirts and jeans, leaving a trail of destruction. I added sweaters, their hangers askew, and sneakers onto the heap.

"Roger said it was here, so it has to be."

Panting, I scanned where I didn't look.

"The bed," I said. "It has to be in bed."

I pushed Howard aside and grabbed his pillow. I yanked off the case, but the zipper snagged, and I ripped it apart. A cloud of down puffed in the air. But that was all it was. Down and fabric, and as the feathers floated to the floor, Howard pinned me to the mattress.

Breathing heavily against me, it had been so long since we found ourselves in this position. Sweating and tired. He was stronger than me.

"Where is it? Please, Howie."

He held me in place. Half in the darkness of the room. With all that I had pulled apart, I still couldn't find the meteorite. I cried for help. But no help was coming.

In time, Howard would release me. And we would clean

the room together, putting everything back in its right place. The room would look like it once did, but it would never be the same.

Mouth pressed into the mattress, I said, "It's my fault."

In those last few seconds, the weight of Howard on me, the weight of the shadows on top of us, I blamed myself. I brought it into this house. The diseased artwork, the meteorite, Gordito, the fear, the secrets. It all bred infection.

When I calmed, I told Howard I needed fresh air.

"Can I trust you?" he asked.

"Yes," I said. "It helps. The air."

He was resistant, but he let me go for a walk.

I called Razi again. I stood in the space between buildings. Vines clinging to the façade. I was among them—ready to be consumed by nature.

"Don't hang up," I said.

A scuffing sound on the other end. The phone scratching back and forth across Razi's chin.

"Why did you say that?" he asked. "About my mother."

"I had no idea," I said. "Not about her."

It wasn't long ago that she lived next door. That we gardened together. That we talked about the joy of the rising sun.

He said, "I knew she was going to do it. She joked about it. But I knew."

"Did she hurt herself?"

"She kept saying she'd rather walk into traffic."

The words were cinder blocks in the conversation. She was witness to her own memory loss. The loss of language. The loss of problem-solving. Severe enough to interfere with her daily life.

"Are you there?" he asked.

How could the same thing happen to both of them? Hundreds of miles apart. Yet, they both ended their lives the same exact way. In the middle of the road.

Like some cruel math equation:

T=60 min
Event 1 – Gordito crossing the road as a car approaches in Portland: $n1$=8 and $t1$=1 min
Event 2 – Sonia steps in front of a bus in Seattle: $n2$=20 and $t2$=0.5 min
P: How likely is it that these events occur within the same 60 minutes?

"I don't know what to say."

Razi said, "You said something about someone you know."

"Gordito," I said.

What else could I say to make him understand? I was calling to tell him about Gordito, to close some loop between the squirrel and Roger, and Sonia and me. But they drifted off without a word. No goodbye. I imagined a light at the end of a long hallway suddenly going dark.

"The squirrel," I finally said. "I found him dead. I wanted to tell her. There's no good way to say this. She named him after your father."

"He wasn't my father."

"I know," I said. "I meant…"

"She technically wasn't really my mother either."

Sonia never said as much.

"If I knew she was sick, I would've helped," I said. "Are you there?"

"I'm here." The words sounded reluctant—untethered. Floating around him like they were winged. "She was worse than I knew. She liked to talk about joy. And nature. But all that was a cover up for the fact that she was depressed. You don't just do something like that. I should've come sooner."

"You can't blame yourself."

I needed to tell him about the meteorite. This was not the

176

act of a woman fighting depression or dealing with dementia. This was something far more powerful.

"Blame myself? I blame you," he said, abruptly. "You saw everything, and you did nothing."

He wouldn't understand; I hardly understood. But if the meteorite had the power to hurt Howard, it certainly had the power to command Sonia into traffic, to command Gordito, too. It had no goal except destruction and to weave its spiderweb of chaos.

I said, "I thought she was sad and tired. That's the honest truth. What I saw was someone without a companion. Maybe I should've called you. But I think she needed someone, and she wasn't going to bother you. So, she took on a pet squirrel, and convinced herself that she found a stone with special powers. Like a charm. Did she show you? Do you have it?"

"Bother me?" He began to breathe faster.

"The stone," I repeated. "Did you see it? A black stone with white… veins."

"How would she bother me?" he said. "I'm all she had."

"She said you had your own life. I think she was too proud to burden you, and maybe I needed someone to need me like that. To rely on me. Maybe that's why it felt bigger, our connection. Your mother was a beautiful person, and I don't think I ever told anyone that until now. But what's more important is the stone. Please tell me you have it. If you have it, Razi, you need to get rid of it. It's not safe."

He was quiet for a long time.

Before anything became violent, there was a pause. The eye of a storm. The silence before the gunshot. Was he going to lash out?

But he sounded calm as he said, "I don't know if you're blaming me, but I don't have regrets. I wish I'd been closer, but I can't blame myself if I didn't know. And when I knew, I did the right thing. I got her help. Not anyone else. Me. I did the right thing."

"I know," I said.

He was right; he was exactly right.

It's strange, I thought. But she had it all. The life, the love. And I was envious, and grateful for the time I had with her. But I didn't help her. Not with all the pain she must've been feeling. Instead, I helped her clean and cook. I wasn't with her like family.

"You're a good son," I said.

I could hear the sadness. The muffled breathing. I imagined him on the other end of the conversation. Hand over his eye, wiping the tears.

He said, "She was a teacher, she taught high school. Did you know?"

I smiled. "I believe it."

"There'll be a memorial," he said. "I'm not sure I do, but she'd want you there."

"I'll be there."

"Sorry about your squirrel," he said.

And I believed that, too.

"Goodbye," I said.

"Wait," he said. "Your stone. We donated everything. But if there was something, it's gone."

Chapter 13

We roamed the city. Aimlessly, turning left or right. Our route passed the Guild of St. Sebastian. I imagined their ghosts—Sonia and Roger—in the bell tower. Together and bodiless forever.

On the sanctuary steps, I said, "Should we hike next weekend? I could use the fresh air. I mean, if your hips are okay."

Howard looked towards the bell tower. I wanted to ask him if he saw them, but he motioned for us to go inside.

"You're joking, right?" I asked. "I know I'm the one who wants us to be more adventurous, but…"

The space smelled of pine and lemon. Our footfalls in the silence made us feel like intruders.

Howard drifted along the wall, gazing at the stained-glass windows; I approached the altar—the echo of each step—and I admired the lectern draped in crimson, a cross the size of a man, the woodwork: intricate spiral dowels weaved within the lattice backdrop. From a time when craft was put on display to honor something greater than the architect.

Then a voice punctuated the peace.

"Can I help you?"

Some essence within me awakened. But the voice didn't come from a bodiless spirit.

The priest emerged from his confessional booth.

"Sorry," I said. "We can leave."

He moved with graceful steps. "Each of us should be sorry, but only for our sins," he said, smiling like a friend.

Howard's gait was more noticeable than ever. The slow turn of his hips.

"Then we'll only be a second," I said, watching Howard enter a pew.

The priest paused. Three crescent wrinkles crossed his

forehead. Howard smiled and knelt. It was a true smile. Then he bowed his head.

The priest said, "I have my doubts about the survival of faith, but here you are. Where did you come from?"

I said, "He's from the Midwest. They all got a healthy dose of Jesus when they were young. But it's been a while for me."

"Like riding a bicycle," the priest said. "Is there a reason for your visit? Maybe confession-curious?"

"We lost someone," I said.

"My condolences," he said. "You've come to the right place." The priest nodded. "If you both ever want to return, we welcome all types. Even Midwesterners, of course. The salt of the earth, as Jesus told his followers in the Sermon on the Mount."

"I think I strayed too far, father." I glanced towards Howard, who was head down in prayer.

"You're always welcome. I shouldn't say this, but we don't have enough handsome men at Sunday service."

My cheeks warmed.

"I appreciate the invite," I said. "Especially from a man in a dress."

The priest laughed loud enough that it pulled Howard from his own stillness. He looked at us. His husband and a priest. If we had our photograph taken, what would be the title?

"I've never thought of it like that," the priest said. "The robes could use an update."

"Regardless," I said. "You look stunning."

"Then I'll see you at service?"

"Probably not, father."

"Robbie," he said. "Call me Robbie."

We walked home on a route we'd traveled a hundred times, exploring what we might've missed. Sometimes it was as simple as looking up instead of down.

"I liked him," I said. "I wasn't expecting that."

Howard could've said I told you so, but he didn't. It was hard to look beyond the obvious. Howard's limp.

"Please call the doctor tomorrow," I said.

He didn't ignore me. He didn't wave me off. Instead, leaned into me.

"Promise?" I asked.

And he squeezed the back of my neck.

Chapter 14

Oregon. A rich, compact slice of the western continent. Nearly a hundred thousand square miles of evergreen woods, lush valleys, snow-peaked mountains, and rolling windswept plains. In a word—majestic. All across the abundant beauty, though, we existed without fully understanding our duty. We were only tenants.

In the yard of our apartment building, Howard dug a shallow hole.

Where the blackberry bushes had been slashed and the tomato vines planted, he picked a few stones from the patch of earth to expose a worm. Curled in his palm, leaving a trail of slippery mucus across his skin, he tossed the worm and wiped his fingers against his thighs.

"Do your hips hurt?"

Howard nodded.

"Did you call?"

He ignored me, so I opened the freezer bag. A smell like cold fresh air. Gordito had been dead for three days and two nights. I emptied the bag. His frozen body tumbled into the pit. He looked tinier, like a rodent. Nothing like a pet.

The wind blew, and a cloud of lilacs fluttered across the grass. I pinched a petal that stuck to my arm, setting it on top of Gordito's head like a skullcap.

"Had another appointment," Howard finally said.

"Why didn't you say so?" I asked.

"Not about my hips."

Oregon. Only a blip of the world in a blip of the galaxy. Still, sparrows cheeped. Crows cawed. And swallows whined and gurgled. This moment in the yard with Howard was to cope with our loss, but nothing around us even paused.

"They ruled out more," Howard said.

"What's next?"

"Another consultation," he said. "A new doctor."

I said, "I feel like there's something you're not telling me."

Howard bent down and cupped fresh soil. Holding it, then exhaling. I knelt beside him.

He said, "I can't do this alone."

"You're not alone," I said. "Do you feel alone?"

A chickadee landed on the wooden fence. It peeped. It looked toward the grave, whistled once. Messengers to the afterlife for their ability to soar to the homes of the gods. But it didn't soar. Instead, it lingered. Our only watcher. Curious about two animals digging a hole.

Watching others do something it didn't understand, I thought.

I was no different. Because even after I stood up, and we began our slow procession back to our apartment, I wasn't any closer to closure.

Chapter 15

I Googled "death rituals." In ancient Egypt, the owners of cats shaved their eyebrows when their pets died. When dogs died, their owners shaved their heads and bodies.

I stood in the shower lathering myself with soap and started with my eyebrows.

Then my face.

My chest.

And armpits.

A sacrificial cleansing. The hair slid from my body, bunching like tumbleweed by the drain, and I lathered my pubic hair. Gently I shaved my testicles and my buttocks, spreading my cheeks and shaving horizontally. My legs were easy, but it took longer. Every nick behind my knees ached like a bee sting when the hot water rinsed the trails of blood.

The bathroom mirror fogged, and I wiped a circle to see myself.

"My god," I said.

No eyebrows. Yet it was still me, my cerulean eyes. That was remarkable. I was alive and had agency. I could shave my head or adopt a baby. It was all life. Random act after random act.

I wore Howard's bathrobe and ate a raisin bagel with butter. Read the news headlines. The president lied in a press conference. Erratic weather patterns on the West Coast. The first commercial trip to the moon had been planned.

Maybe all these random acts added up to this present moment. I took great relief in knowing that I had honored Gordito. It was my way of saying goodbye and beginning anew. Like a child born into the world, hairless and alert, so too was I. If we were going to take this next step to start a family, I needed this perspective. Everything was in its right place.

Howard arrived home, opened the door. Terror in his eyes.

"The Egyptians did it," I said. "But I'm better. And I'm ready."

He pressed his face into my neck and gasped. Noise with emotion. And inside the noise, a flood of intensity.

"It's okay," I said, and stroked the back of his head. "It'll grow back. I promise. All the hair will return. Like springtime. That's what we want. Need. A new birth. This is just my way of getting there. Emotionally. Do you understand? I couldn't get there before, but I know we're safe now. Nothing is holding us back anymore."

But I knew he wasn't pressing against me because I had been reborn. While I was trying to tap into some ancient understanding of death and birth, Howard was dealing with his own great struggle. He was clinging to me to keep something beautiful from slipping away.

Chapter 16

I was on edge. Too much coffee. Trying to read an essay by Sartre—a story of prisoners awaiting their execution. Throughout the night, one by one, the prisoners were led away until only one remained. In the morning, he was spared.

But the prisoner had prepared all night long to welcome the firing squad's bullets, the ammunition like hot coals ripping through his flesh.

He was pardoned because of a lie he'd told his captors about the location of his network—criminals on the run. He was trying to protect them, but they were at the exact place of his lie. All arrested, all sentenced to death.

In some ways, life never made sense. Random act followed by random act. Yet we try to give them all meaning. And structure. To find a pattern when none existed. Sonia was dead, and Gordito was dead. What did that mean?

The memorial for Sonia was crowded. Family, friends, acquaintances shoulder to shoulder. She spent her early years in Port Townsend, so it was fitting her family and friends would remember her at the Uptown Pub in the center of the city.

I wondered how to snake through the crowd to order a drink. I shouldn't drink. But I needed a whiskey.

Port Townsend, where Sonia had first lived—after her parents immigrated from Syria—was founded as a shipping port in the late 1800s, but now investors from Los Angeles and Seattle renovated the Victorian homes and rented them to tourists.

Razi called only moments before our drive to Port Townsend. He asked if I wanted to speak toward the end of the service. All attendees would be given a chance, he'd said, and at the last minute, he remembered he had forgotten us.

"It really shouldn't be more than a few minutes," he'd said

on the phone.

"I'd love a couple minutes," I'd said. "If you wouldn't mind."

"It's the least I could do."

The memorial service focused on stories about her during different points in her life, told to an audience of loved ones and a framed picture of Sonia on an easel.

Most of the stories were funny. If I could see her now, I'd see the mirth in her eyes. A flicker like a flash of gold pebbles in a stream. Stories teasing her of her clumsiness or her obsession with Korean romance novels. No one told any story about her walking in front of a bus. Instead, they stuck to stories of her years as a schoolteacher or volunteer at the animal shelter. For almost two hours we listened to story after story, and then the microphone was handed to me.

"Me?" I asked, as Razi offered me the opportunity.

"She'd have wanted it," he said.

I looked at Howard, and nothing about him said I shouldn't.

I cleared my throat, but the sound amplified across the room.

"Sorry," I said, and the audience nodded.

"I'm not really sure what to say," I said. "I'm Thom, and well, I was Sonia's neighbor in Portland."

I held the microphone away, and I cleared my throat, again.

Howard took my hand, and I was sure he would take the microphone, too. But he did not release me, just squeezed my hand three times. I didn't need to give every one of them context because I wasn't speaking to them.

Starting over, I said, "Sonia, you were an inspiration. When your Roger died, you had the courage to get out of bed; I'm not sure I could."

I glanced at Howard.

"I'm here with my husband, and I can say when he dies, it'll crush me. Sorry to be morbid, honey. But it didn't crush you,

Sonia. It showed you how to see the world. How to love what you still have. Friends and memories."

They all agreed. A few people raised their glasses in the air.

"Don't misunderstand," I continued. "That's what she found when she left this place. Sonia warned me; she said her old friends talked about her behind her back. Things about Roger. She felt like an outsider here. But you didn't know Sonia. Not really, because she left this place so she could be herself. That's what she told me. I don't even think her son knew her the way I knew her. But that's what I'm here to tell you. You still have time to get to know the people right next to you."

Razi wound his way back through the snug crowd. He was polite, walking calmly, not swinging his elbows. Another man would've shoved people, yelled, cussed. Teeth showing. Not grinning but growling.

I smiled at the framed picture of Sonia.

"But Roger, your second husband, he made you happy. I could see it in the way you talked about him. And when he died, you told me his memories were what kept you going. You saw him in everything that was left. His coffee mug that you drank from. Even in the garden. You saw him there beside me. Now I understand, because I see you. And I realize it doesn't have to end."

The crowd around me wore expressionless masks because that was appropriate when someone was talking about you. We were in a space with rules. Memorials were meant for introspection, not rebellion.

"That's enough," Razi said, grabbing at the mic.

"You said a few minutes."

Howard tugged at my elbow.

"That's fine. I said what I needed to say," I told Razi. "Most of us will never know what it's like to be free. But she finally found her peace of mind. I'm sorry if that hurts."

"Get out of here," Razi said.

Howard pulled me through the crowd; I was ecstatic, and I said, "None of us are dead yet. We still have time. Wake up! Wake up and live."

And there she was standing at the door grinning. Sonia reached out and touched my wrist. It was only for a moment. Something like a voice traveling from her to me. A message through contact.

"It's not gone," the message said.

"What's not?" I asked.

"The meteorite," she said.

From the sidewalk, I could no longer see her.

"Where?" I called, but there was no one to ask.

An empty sidewalk in a city on a peninsula. The breeze blew from the Puget Sound and grabbed my words, pulling them to the sea. The flat surface of that body of water offered few obstacles. No trees or rocks or buildings. Words moving without interruption. Where were they going? And who would hear them?

Chapter 17

We arrived early for Howard's appointment. At his last one, all the usual tests: blood pressure, heart rate, temperature, auscultation. No X-rays unless Howard thought it would give him peace.

They recommended he come back again. And then again.

Dr. Rao wore red glasses—too large for her face. Her quiet voice comforted me. I had no idea what Howard was thinking, but he appeared calm. No tension in his cheeks. Dr. Rao clicked her mouse and then opened a file on her computer.

"We've never felt more important," I said. "Thanks for seeing us so quickly. I'll give you a good Yelp review."

Dr. Rao didn't look up.

"I'm kidding," I said, and glanced at Howard, who continued staring straight ahead.

Dr. Rao scanned one lab after another. "Your sedimentation is subnormal, which typically means an infection is present."

"What do you mean an infection?" I asked.

Howard squeezed my knee.

I said, "If you're not going to ask, I am."

Dr. Rao removed her glasses, rubbing her nose.

"The pain in your hips, the lethargy," Dr. Rao said, looking at Howard. "I'd like to run a few more tests. If it's alright with you?"

"What do they cost?" I interrupted.

Howard turned.

"I know, I know," I said, pushing back into my chair.

Dr. Rao said, "This shouldn't be a conversation about cost. If you understand. The sooner we can run the tests the better."

"What kind of tests?" Howard asked, covering the side of his mouth with his hand.

"A prostate exam to start," she said. "Additional blood tests, if necessary. But we can start today."

"Is that a routine exam?" I asked. "The prostate one?"

"We have to rule everything out," Dr. Rao said. "The previous tests tell me we have to run more tests. Do you both understand?"

Was this a part of the pattern?

"Is everything connected?" I asked. "What about his face? Is that part of it?"

"No," Dr. Rao said. "I don't think the intermittent facial paralysis has anything to do with this. But what we must focus on now is what's immediate. And that's more tests."

"Is it serious?" I asked. "Like cancer serious?"

"We need to rule everything out," Dr. Rao repeated.

"But it could be?" Howard asked. "It could be that serious?"

"Right now, I can only say that more tests are needed."

A week passed. Waiting was the expectation. You wait and you go about your life like you're not thinking about it every other moment.

Howard received an automated phone message from the hospital that his test results had been returned from the lab. He called the clinic, spoke to a shift nurse.

I could hear her say, "A mass."

"A mass of what?" Howard asked. "Of cancer?"

I grabbed his shirt sleeve. "You have cancer?"

"A biopsy."

Imagine an endless thread of red yarn tied around every moment in time from the past into the future. Follow that yarn from one instance to the next, as if it was the only route we could ever take. And for all the ups and downs, the glorious triumphs and rainy-day blues, that red yarn always leads to this end.

Positively cancer.

Chapter 18

The door at Floyd's Coffee Shop chimed. Someone in, someone out. Rain beaded on the window. Cars and bicycles passed. People with problems. Repeating scenes. I picked a raisin from my bagel, and let the sweetness soften against my tongue.

At the table behind me, a couple talked about their weekend. They weren't a couple-couple. She told him a story about meeting a woman who was bad for her. Brought her home anyway. Never called after that, but she didn't care.

"I mean, not really," the woman explained. "I was using her, too."

Her friend, the man, nodded. "At least you had a good time."

"Sure. It was fun," she said. "But still. What's it all really mean?"

"Everything doesn't always mean something," he said. "Who said that?"

"Should we get a drink?" she asked.

He raised his half empty coffee cup.

"I mean a real drink," she said. "I'm depressed."

As I listened to them, I scribbled on an article in the newspaper. Blacking out words.

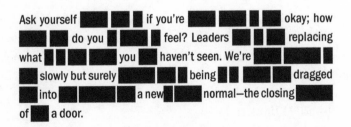

Ask yourself ▮▮ ▮ if you're ▮▮ ▮▮ ▮ okay; how ▮▮ do you ▮ ▮ feel? Leaders ▮ ▮ replacing what ▮ ▮▮ you ▮ haven't seen. We're ▮ ▮▮ slowly but surely ▮▮ ▮ being ▮ ▮ ▮ dragged ▮ into ▮ ▮ a new▮ ▮ normal—the closing ▮▮ of ▮ a door.

I'd spent so much time looking into other people's lives: Kit and Lenni, Sonia, my parents, Howard. Why did I watch others so closely? To understand how it all worked? Life? Living? But even after all that, here I am. Still wondering. Still grasping. Nothing I saw prepared me for this.

I folded the newspaper in half and walked home.

At the corner of Morrison and 17th, a man standing at the bus stop asked for spare change. His eyes were blood-flecked. A timeworn face. When he walked, he was unsteady on his feet. His green Army jacket was moth-eaten, and protruding from his right long sleeve, you could see two crooked fingers. Maybe an old sports injury.

"Best time for change is right now."

"Sorry," I said. "Spent it on the paper."

"It's all bad news."

He had a friendly smile.

"Can I ask you something?"

"For a dollar seventy-five," he said.

I handed him two bucks, and he grabbed it with his crooked hand.

"What makes you happy?"

He laughed so hard I almost joined him. He took a few steps back and turned like he was going to leave, but then he faced me.

"That's what you want to know? That's worth more than two bucks."

"Okay," I said, and gave him another dollar bill.

"Three bucks," he said. "You can't buy nothing with three bucks. But me, three bucks is happiness. Three amazing bucks. You understand?"

Perspective, I thought.

I said, "I think so."

"Yeah," he said. "Me too."

He didn't say anything else.

There was an empty future that played out in my mind as I walked home. Until now, I didn't want to be a father. But I didn't want to do it alone either. In our marriage, we took a long time to understand one another. Despair. Distress. Fear. Rage.

Each of us was born facing the same direction, and from that moment, every step we stepped, every breath we breathed, every turn we made—we all moved closer to the end of life.

That I knew.

There would be no family; there would be no adoption.

That I also knew.

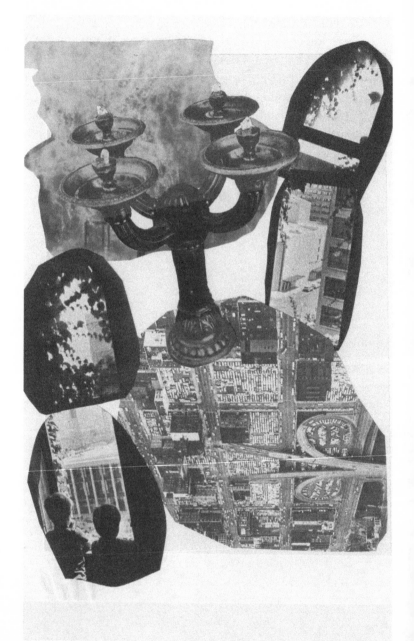

Chapter 19

"You look awful."

Howard in bed, skin almost gray. How long had this been going on? Months? His treatments meant he wasn't eating much.

In the beginning, the weight loss was slow—two or three pounds—but then it increased rapidly. The sight of a skeletal human brings to mind all those photos of concentration camp prisoners. Their jutting, rippled sternums under tightened skin. But this was Howard. The hollowness of his chest and the tendons in his neck. Signs of his deterioration.

"But still beautiful," I clarified.

He had endured three rounds of chemo. Aocetaxel, cabazitaxel, and mitoxantrone. And while they slowed the growth, the tumor didn't shrink.

I crossed the room. "The doctor said you're on the mend now."

He thought for a moment.

"Are you worried?"

I pulled him close, his shoulder blades against my chest. I rubbed his back in large circles and felt the bones in his back pushing through his skin. He bowed. I ran my hands through the few hairs that remained on his head.

"You're twitching," I said.

He took a deep breath.

I said, "This would be a terrible movie. No one would watch it, and I like sad movies."

"Not unless we were goldfish," he said.

"Cartoon goldfish maybe."

He laughed. Or gasped.

I thought of the squirrel and the mountain. Neither of us could carry a forest on our back, but we could still crack a nut.

That little bit of power was enough to remind me it was not over. Not yet.

Chapter 20

Ghosts of sleep haunted my vision; I thought I'd woken up into a past life. Howard's face half-sunken into his pillow. He looked like a younger version of himself. Howard disguised as Howard. Both eyes. A beautiful mouth. That smile.

I ran my finger along his lips. But this was not real. A black cat sat in the corner of the room watching us.

I opened my eyes again. A garbage truck passed our apartment; the windows rattled. Howard pulled the sheet over his head, covering his eye, his closed mouth.

I stared at myself in the bathroom mirror, but the man in the mirror was not me. He had my face and cerulean eyes, but that man was about to drive his husband to the hospital. That was not my future; that was not me. It was a film neither one of us had asked to see.

I said, "Today's going to happen whether we like it or not."

Howard couldn't eat or drink. He watched me toast a cinnamon raisin bagel, spread a gob of butter along the surface, liquid pooling then absorbing.

He wore my flannel shirt.

"You look tough," I said, half-laughing. "Lewis and Clark wore flannel. And today you're going to wear it."

He looked lost. Cheeks sunken, eyes tired, red.

Nodding, I said, "Or maybe Lewis and Clark wore raccoon pelts. But you know what I mean. You're ready for an adventure."

I wondered what his doctor was doing that very moment. Was she fighting with her husband while sitting at the breakfast table? Was she thinking about her daily schedule? Thinking about all the patients on her list? Maybe she was measuring out oatmeal for her daughter's breakfast or walking their labradoodle around the neighborhood while she smoked a menthol cigarette—only one a day—because sanity through moderate vices was a life philosophy she was okay with. Even a doctor could believe that. Was she thinking about her colleagues? Was she thinking about how many families she had seen torn apart by cancer?

By now, she must see people as objects—machines in need of parts when broken. But maybe that was a good thing. Removing emotion removed fear of failure.

I told myself, *Breathe in, feel strong.* I had no reason to think anything would go wrong. I read that salvage prostatectomies were less complex than other extractions. Still, into the cosmos I sent positivity. Not prayers.

I lifted my chin:

Dear Universe. The doctor is going to wake up rested, and the nurses too. The general anesthesia will be peaceful, and Howard will dream like a baby, all jubilant. Everyone will notice him smiling in his sleep.

Chapter 21

As we drove to the hospital, I played one of Howard's favorite songs by Townes Van Zandt. Howard made me listen to it the morning we got married, told me he'd always imagined it would be his wedding song. He'd said that it was written from a dream.

But now, Howard turned off the radio.

"You love that song," I said.

"I can't," he said.

All I wanted was for today to be over—to wake up tomorrow next to him and say, "I told you we had nothing to worry about."

Crossing the parking lot, I said hello to every person: doctors, nurses, surgeons, and strangers. I needed karma.

The hospital hallways rattled with coughs and prayers.

We sat beside an old man. Obese and as ripe as cumin, hooked up to a green respirator tank on wheels. Beside him a teenage girl holding a bag of frozen blueberries to her nose. But they weren't together. The girl sat with her mother, a woman in sunglasses, who flinched every time her daughter repositioned the bag as if the pain jumped from person to person.

We would wait until Howard's name was called.

"How do you feel?" I asked him. "Waiting is strange. We do it like it's normal. But none of this is normal. We're all sitting here, not saying a word, like everything will be alright. Do you want me to get you a Snapple or something?"

He looked tired. Eyes low, head down. Even if he wasn't up all night, he wasn't rested either.

I said, "It'll be over soon."

The nurse finally called Howard's name. We stood in unison.

I said, "I'll see you soon, peanut butter." I handed him off to the nurse. "Take good care of him. He's an original, and you can't get 'em like that anymore."

The nurse said, "I'll treat him like he's my own."

They moved through the swinging doors, and through the glass I watched them until they turned a corner. Someone had already taken my seat. A man who held his face in his hands. He sobbed, muttering, "Oh, Roxy."

Between his fingers, his entire nose looked missing. Blood clotted in the gap.

"Shh," the woman beside him said. She rubbed his back in small circles.

I lingered a few minutes. Everyone seemed so much worse than Howard. That felt good.

Outside, I paced the sidewalk. An elderly couple sat on a bench. They tried to hold themselves upright but kept tipping over at the waist. I nodded, and the man tried to grin. Simply sitting upright was a struggle, and I knew how much I took for granted.

I returned to the waiting room. Aimlessly flipped through a car magazine, and another about parenting, and another about global catastrophes.

After an hour, my stomach ached. I wasn't about to leave the hospital, leave Howard. I found a vending machine one floor up. All that candy and soda. I scanned the drinks, spotting a bottle of Snapple. I bought it, twisted off the cap.

There are one million ants to every human in the world.

I thought of all the caps Howard had saved. Random facts he stored in his mind for trivia night when our lives were routine.

I bought five more bottles.

A honeybee can fly at 15 mph.
Cats have over 100 vocal cords.
Camel's milk does not curdle.

A jellyfish is 95% water.

If I could find the right one, maybe it would be over—maybe I could hit reset and get back to a place of normalcy.

A nurse passed me. "Thirsty?"

"I'm trying to win the sweepstakes," I said.

"Make sure to share it with me."

I twisted the next cap and read aloud, "Fish cough."

Those words. I spent my entire life not planning a future, but the year it felt organic, this happened. Cancer and this phrase. Why couldn't I read it to him right now?

Two hours passed. I asked the receptionist for an update, but she told me it looked like Howard was still in surgery.

"When that changes, hon, you'll be the first to know."

I read and reread the bottle cap in my mind.

Fish cough.
Fish cough.
Fish cough.

It felt hopeful. Life was easier the last time I said those words to Howard. There was a promise in the phrase. Coughing something from the body. It was a brief interruption before carrying onwards.

Fish cough, but then they continue to live.

Chapter 22

I finally heard my name. At ten minutes past four, the receptionist ushered Dr. Rao to me. I smiled but seeing her felt off. It was the first time in a long time I knew in my bones I was not as strong as I thought.

She held her arms across her chest.

"What?" I asked. "It was a routine surgery. That's what everyone said."

Her words were soft, floating, unattached to her or this room or this world.

She explained what *complications* meant. How the bleeding started immediately, but when she tied off the bleeding vessel the same thing happened again. The vein walls weakened over time, she said, by the mass.

"When do I see him?" I asked. "Is he waiting?"

There was so much to process. But I knew if I could just see him that everything would be alright. I would read him the Snapple cap.

But then she held up a stone. A small black stone. White veins pulsing through the hard surface.

She said, "He asked me to give this to you."

Her words were small. Like she was speaking from another room.

The world began to spin: the ceiling, the walls, the tile floor. A spinning dreidel. Colors, textures blending. Everything was gray and frothy. Then I was standing in the center of an empty plain. Dead volcanoes, impact craters, and lava flows. I looked down at myself. I wasn't there. Only vision without form.

My legs gave out beneath me, and I collapsed onto the cold tile floor. I couldn't move. I didn't want to move. I wanted to sink into the floor until I was entirely swallowed whole.

Take me great beast of the unknown.

I looked up at her, so high above me. Who was she, and why was she doing this to me?

"So, that's it?" I asked. "He's dead?"

"Dead?"

"Howard," I said.

"No," she said. "But he's not out of the woods; he lost a lot of blood. We need to keep him overnight, maybe longer."

"But he'll live?" I asked.

"He's stable," she said.

The words lifted me from the floor.

"He's alive," she repeated. "But he asked me to hold onto this for you."

How did she have the meteorite?

"He said it was a good luck charm," Dr. Rao repeated. "I told him I'd keep it safe until he was out of surgery."

He'd had it all along, I thought. *And he never told me.*

Chapter 23

Howard sat awake. There was something odd about the way he looked at me. His face changed. Not worse. Everything moving back into its right place.

I sat on the chair by his bed, and he looked disappointed.

"I can't believe it," I said.

"I can't either," he said.

"How do you feel?"

"I don't know."

"You don't have to say anything," I said.

"They said I can leave in a few days."

"Then I'll camp right here," I said.

"Don't be stupid," he said, coughing.

From the nightstand, I handed him a glass of water. He drank slowly through the straw.

"There's no reason we both have to suffer at the hospital."

"She gave it to me," I said.

"I'm sorry," Howard said.

"Why did you hide it?"

"I don't know," he said. "It didn't make sense. But then I knew what you were talking about. What it was doing."

I said, "You have no idea. I thought I lost you, Howie. I don't know what I'd do without you."

"Come here," he said, but he was too tired to spread his arms. When I hugged him, he pressed his face against my face. *The way his hair smells*, I thought.

"Now do you believe me?" I asked.

I could feel his grip around me. Lightly. But there. He was right there.

"When you get home," I said. "We can …"

"Shh," he said. "No promises."

"Okay," I said. "Okay."

Chapter 24

An ornament of horror.

I don't know how long I sat in the dark staring at the meteorite on the kitchen table. Without a siren or a roar or a knock at the door. No hiss, or rattle, or gunshot percussion. No scent. No blood. That was how it arrived. Suddenly. Quietly.

But noise filled my mind. Everything in our apartment told a story. The books on his nightstand. The shoes in his closet. The socks in our laundry basket. The box of ginger tea. The tissues in the wastebasket. Artifacts from our life together. But this *thing*. It was trying to destroy all that.

Shadows in the room shifted with the sun. My stomach gurgled.

When did we buy the Muybridge photograph? How old was Howard when he etched the boy and the woman? Or did I make that print? Did he like Bonnie "Prince" Billy? I couldn't remember ever listening to a song together. There was that one—what were the lyrics?

And then I see a darkness. Did you know how much I love you? Can you save me from this darkness?

I remembered some trips we'd taken. To Netarts Bay and our anniversary in San Francisco. I couldn't remember if he gave a toast at dinner, or did I? We did go to Netarts Bay, right? I was sure it had all happened. The memories blurred, and I had no one to tell me if one was right or another was wrong.

I began to wonder if everything in the world had died. I was too lazy to go to the window and look. Were the flowers still blooming? Had the birds stopped singing? Was the sun even burning? Was the meteorite doing all this to me? Making me think like this.

I Googled "How to destroy a meteorite?" The only results were science fiction films about the end of the world.

I couldn't just throw it out. It would always find its way back. I needed to pulverize the stone. Somehow blast it into smithereens. Then I found a blog about drilling through rocks.

"Best on the market," Dad had said about the Makita he'd bought for Howard. "Drill through anything."

I knew what I had to do.

I dug out the drill from the closet and charged its battery. I held the black stone firmly and found a groove. That was where I'd start. I pulled the trigger of the drill, and the bit immediately twisted off the stone. I tried again, pressing harder.

The bit spun in place. I blew away the metal shavings, and after a minute there was smoke. When I stopped, the bit was ground down. Only half the length.

I unlocked the chuck and replaced the bit with another one. But the meteorite fought back. Glowing and burning. Destroying bit after bit. An invincible creature from another world. Meteorites were made of iron and nickel, nothing that could not be cracked. But this one was different.

That night, I bought new bits. Steel. Titanium. And carbide. But I had a feeling about the outcome—the meteorite was composed of something much stronger. Some knowledge from another world captured within its core. And until I knew its opposite, I couldn't restore any balance.

I spent the next morning on the meteorite. No matter the material, the meteorite won.

When the last bit broke, it was like being shot in the chest by a cannonball. Torso blown away, strewn across a field on fire.

This is the end, I thought.

If I couldn't destroy it, it would destroy us.

Is that the balance that this ornament of horror was seeking?

I don't know how long I sat there staring at the meteorite. Sipping coffee from my farmer's market mug. An unassuming mug. Brown glaze exterior, but it was the inside that had originally caught my attention. Galactic swirls of variegated blue formed a small universe of color. It amused Howard to use this mug. Over time, I stopped caring if he broke it. I only cared that it was in good hands—his hands. The mug had come to symbolize our story together.

He would return home in two days, which meant I had one more day to figure out how to destroy the meteorite.

I slammed the mug on top of the meteorite. A fierce bang. The galactic blue swirls flying in all directions. Only the handle was left. Is that how the potter begins, with a handle of something?

Chapter 25

The sun through the stained-glass windows cast a prism of immaterial planets. Pink and purple and orange orbs of light against the walls.

I sat in the last pew, hoping an answer would emerge. Some secret narrative that I could follow to explain the patterns of life. I had taken to wearing Howard's clothes—his jeans too long, shirt too bulky. But the extra room felt like space saved for him. Part of me prepared for the worst, even though Howard was supposed to come home.

Father Robbie said, "I remember you."

"I didn't mean to interrupt," I said.

"If you're praying, you're staying." He set his hand on my shoulder.

"That's clever." His hand was warm. It smelled nice, like soap. "Did you think of that?"

"We hired an agency to help us appeal to the younger generations. That's the best they came up with."

"Did it work?"

"You get what you pay for," he said, looking around the empty sanctuary. "Our budget was small, but we're praying."

He sat beside me; together we faced the altar. It made it easier—not looking at him.

"Can I pray with you?" he asked.

"I'm having trouble getting started," I said. "I don't know how to say it, but there's something wrong. Wrong's not the right word. Maybe … cursed."

"Cursed?"

"I know how it sounds," I said. "I'm a little nervous. You see for a while I had this idea that objects influence us. I'm not explaining it right."

"Take your time."

"Do you believe in evil?" I asked.

Father Robbie said, "Curses we don't do, but evil is our specialty."

If we were playing poker, he'd win. His face never changed. In fact, he seemed curious to hear more.

"Can I ask what kind of evil?"

"From another place," I said. "Somewhere unknown."

"Interesting." He squinted one eye. "Yes, I do believe in evil, and its opposite. It's part of the job to usher people toward goodness."

"I'm not talking about people," I said. "But a *thing*. Like an evil stone."

"My mentor used to ask me questions like this," he said. "It takes me back."

"I'm serious," I said.

"As am I," Father Robbie said. "And just like I used to respond to Father Vincent, good and evil is often what we make of it. You ask about a stone, and yes, a stone can be evil. An opal, for instance, can be evil if we say it's evil. Black opals are thought to be extremely unlucky in some cultures. While I might not assign it as evil, I can't say if someone else shouldn't. Maybe I'm not answering your question."

"I think you are," I said. "A stone can be evil if we say it is. But what if *it* just is, no matter what people think?"

"When I woke up, I never thought I'd be having this conversation," Father Robbie said. "But I enjoy these types of talks. So, I'll tell you what I know. If something is bad, then we know it's bad because there is something good in comparison. Your stone, the evil one, what if you had one that was good? Could it cancel out the other?"

"I never thought of that."

"Diamonds are good stones, just so you know," he said. "This isn't the advice of the church. You understand? This is because I know a few things about stones. I shouldn't be telling you this, but I have a crystal altar. The way the light hits them. It's truly glorious."

I said, "I have my mother's engagement ring. But it's tiny."

"Size doesn't matter," he said, winking. "Marry the two. And *voila*."

I shifted my weight, and the wooden bench creaked.

"And the evil is gone?" I asked.

"With the help of something good, yes," he said.

Father Robbie turned his body towards mine and gestured at the stained-glass windows: scenes from two thousand years ago. "These scenes are not the scenes of today. I watch the news. I see it, so we can't hold culture hostage because of what it said back then. But love is the core message… then and now. That's what's important, because that holds the future in place. If there is something evil, surround it with love. That's the only way. It's a message as old as time."

"I've never met anyone like you," I said. "Show it love."

"It should always be about love. But we all love differently and sometimes love gets corrupted. It leads to exclusion. Or war. Or pain. That's our flaw as humans. That's how the evil manifests in the first place. But that doesn't change the core. If we can remind ourselves of that, even when we falter, then there's hope that love will bring us back."

"That's why I'm here."

"We have that in common," he said. "That's why I show up every day."

I thought about good and evil and crystal altars and positive energy and negative energy and Sky and Howard and the things we surround ourselves with and what I had to do. The pattern was negation. Cancel one with another.

"I need to go," I said. "There's one last thing to try."

"Remember love," Father Robbie said.

Chapter 26

Dawn's cold air orbited the apartment. I couldn't see it, but it was there. Meanwhile I was alive in our bed in our room. Thinking. Planning. When I opened my eyes, I knew that life was not as artless as waking and dying. Something strange moved inside me, nestling in my chest.

I lay in bed, but this energy pushed through me. It was time to get up and go.

If it didn't work, I would have nothing except memories. Kissing Howard the very first time. Saying I love you too quickly. Him crawling on his hands and knees across the floor to hold Gordito. Reading "fish cough" to him and listening to the rest of his Snapple caps. Deciding to start a family. All with Howard. All for love.

For so long I thought fish cough was a noun—a thing in the air, but Howard assured me it was an act. The impersonation of our own struggles.

Fish cough like I cough; fish smile like I smile. Fish love like I love, like we loved—Howard and me.

In the end, there were no boundaries to our relationship. We kept learning about one another, about life and death and pleasure and sadness and ourselves—animals really, trying to make sense of all this chaos.

But it was simple.

Fish talk like we talk. Like we laugh. Like we live.

We woke up day after day believing it could get better.

Sky arrived a little before nine. I wore Howard's bathrobe and stood between the buildings where the fat-capped blackberries ripened, and the round red tomatoes bulged.

"I never would've guessed all this," Sky said. "But I'm glad you told me. It's important you don't do this alone."

The simple beauty of nature, Father Robbie told me before

I left, was proof that God existed.

I couldn't say for certain.

"Someone I trust brought up diamonds," I said to Sky. "I think it's the only option I have."

On my knees, I dug a hole. Sky handed me a white cotton pouch. The meteorite and the engagement ring together.

She clapped her hands once. "We seek protection," she said. "We block negativity and all that is wrong."

I let go of the white sack. The meteorite and the engagement ring in the hole.

The apartment would be sold off, the building torn down. The lot excavated. New concrete, rebar, steel pillars. The forthcoming sight of a monolith—fifteen stories at least—for future people.

The two stones in a hole imprisoned and protected. Yin and yang.

I patted the mound and rubbed my fingers into the soil. Dirt under my nails, I pushed again into the earth.

"This is where it all started." Sky took off her larimar necklace.

"Fate," I said. "Who knows, right?"

"The beginning and the ending," she said, offering me the necklace. "All the time."

I took a deep breath and closed my eyes. The red darkness. Phosphenes glowing like the stars. A world unknown but closer than any place else. When I looked deeper, I saw my past. Sonia and Roger and Gordito. I saw the charred oak tree. My mother and father driving me to the animal shelter, where I'd pick out Casey. I saw my whole life. Every place I've ever been. The Adirondacks to Alaska. My mother's diamond engagement ring. The way the stone glinted when I wore it as a child and when I set it next to the meteorite in the white cotton pouch. And right now. Sky by my side offering me her larimar.

I saw the future, too. Howard coming home. The look of relief. It was him again—Howard's face. And I saw the two of us. Much older. Wrinkled and holding onto one another as we walked. There was no beginning or end. Time moving in all directions. A life driven by mysterious powers. We gave all of it meaning. But we can take that meaning away, too.

I exhaled.

Fish cough.